More novels by Simon Mundy:
Silent Movements
Flagey in Autumn
The Fragile Land

Non-fiction:
Making it Home: Europe and the Politics of Culture

Poetry:
Letter to Carolina
By Fax to Alice Springs
After the Games
More for Helen of Troy
Waiting for Music
Blue Med: Selected Poems

Flagey in Winter

SIMON MUNDY

illustrated by
EWGENIYA LYRAS

HAY PRESS

HAY PRESS
10 High Town
Hay-on-Wye
HR3 5AE

an imprint of

RENARD PRESS LTD
124 City Road, London EC1V 2NX
United Kingdom

info@renardpress.com
020 8050 2928
www.haypress.co.uk

Flagey in Winter first published by Hay Press in 2024

Text © Simon Mundy, 2024
Illustrations © Ewgeniya Lyras, 2024

Cover design by Will Dady

Printed on FSC-accredited papers in the UK by 4edge Limited

ISBN: 978-1-80447-093-0

9 8 7 6 5 4 3 2 1

Simon Mundy asserts his moral right to be identified as the author of this work in accordance with the Copyright, Designs and Patents Act 1988.

This is a work of fiction. Any resemblance to actual persons, living or dead, is purely coincidental, or is used fictitiously.

CLIMATE POSITIVE   Renard Press is proud to be a climate positive publisher, removing more carbon from the air than we emit and planting a small forest. For more information see renardpress.com/eco.

All rights reserved. This publication may not be reproduced, stored in a retrieval system or transmitted, in any form or by any means – electronic, mechanical, photocopying, recording or otherwise – without the prior permission of the publisher.

FLAGEY IN WINTER

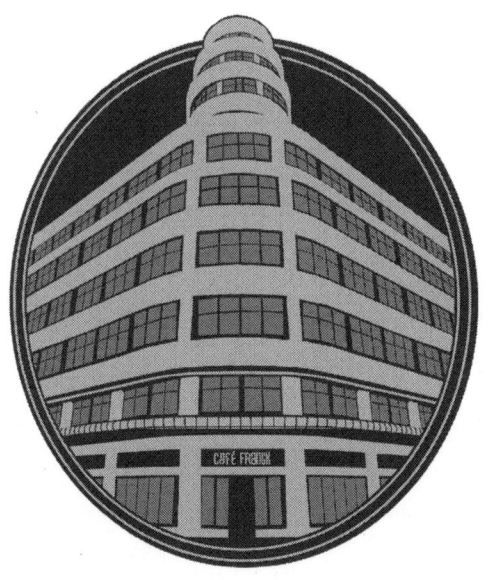

*This story is set in 2013, before governments in so much of Europe
began to behave even more obnoxiously than usual*

Who Is Who

Principal Characters

Catrina	Assistant to Gwyneth Price MEP
Patrice	A barman in Café Franck, Flagey
Damien	Another barman in the same
Elise	A student and barwoman in the same
'Fidel' van de Looy	An occasional professor
Nikita	A gallery owner
Mercedes	Nikita's assistant
Rory McBain	A journalist
Agnestina	A student
Flamand	A poetic student
Artur	Elise's brother
Tyron Wangstrutt	An American lobbyist
Bruno Inchcombe	Assistant to Tony Sanderson MEP
Mariana	Assistant to Esko Nystrom MEP
Saskia van Katwijk	Assistant to a Dutch MEP
Gwyneth Price	An MEP from Wales
Roberto Vincenzi	An MEP from Italy
Esko Nystrom	An MEP from Finland
Leontios	An MEP from Greece
Amelie Poitiers	A French film star
Lucia Redetti	An EU commissioner

Previously...

*as they say
in all transatlantic drama series*

...*in* Flagey in Autumn

Catrina bumped into Mercedes and annoyed Saskia, moved jobs in the European Parliament, dumped Bruno and acquired Patrice. Esko became a political leader, though reluctantly, and was surprised by film star Amelie. Roberto sidled away. Mariana did things she regretted. Nikita hired Mercedes to help in her gallery. Flamand and Agnestina fell in and out of love. Fidel fumed and found Elise.

I

Sunday

First Thing

The sixth of January was always going to be a head-under-the-duvet sort of day. For a start (which most people wished it hadn't), it was freezing in Brussels, with a bitter north-westerly driving a mixture of sleet and spiky snow against any window foolish enough to open curtains to it. Christmas and good cheer had long since dissipated (except for the ex-pat Russians, for whom it was Christmas Eve), and among the Scots, Hogmanay hangovers had just about made their final retreat. The only good thing about it was that it was a Sunday.

Catrina's head was as firmly under the duvet as it was possible to get without suffocating. She would have liked the cover to have been supplemented by the comforting contours of her Belgian barman, Patrice, but it wasn't. He had left to start the coffee machines at Café Franck at the corner of the Flagey arts building before the light crept up. Instead Catrina had to make do with the limited support of her sturdy English hot-water bottles, now warming her with less power than she would have liked.

Cradling the flannel and rubber against her chest, she wondered whether it was worth emerging from the dark and risking the chill long enough to boil a kettle. The advantage was that she could come back to bed with a refreshed bottle and a mug of tea. The disadvantage was that she might shiver to death in the process. A glance at the Big Ben alarm clock by the bedside light told her it was nine-thirty. No need to rush, then.

Catrina transferred the warmer of the two water bottles to her feet. It didn't help much. Something was going to have to give because, in this state somewhere between colder in bed and frozen out of it, she couldn't even daydream straight. From somewhere deep in her psyche Catrina's Derbyshire Peak District ancestors were telling her in disgusted voices not to be so soft. She was bloody lucky to have a sheet, let alone a duvet – and if her feet were cold she should put three pairs of socks on. Catrina groaned and, not for the first time in her twenty-three years, told the ancestors to piss off.

They took umbrage, but they had a minor victory too. Catrina grimaced and swung her feet out of bed and straight into her furry Pussy-Cat slippers, grabbed a jumper from the floor, flicked the switch on the electric heater and stumbled to the tiny kitchen. Once the kettle was filled and heating she ran back to bed. Maybe the ancestors were right about the socks. She wished she'd had the sense to bring the thick woollen hill-walking ones from home back with her to Brussels after the Christmas holiday. It was true they'd never fit in any of her town work shoes, but just now they'd be toe savers.

An hour and a half later the room had warmed sufficiently for Catrina to have progressed through the tea, snooze and shower stages to actually being dressed: leggings, jeans, T-shirt, two jumpers, two pairs of socks, at least, and scarf. Outside the weather remained discouraging – if not quite a reason for total inaction.

The trouble was that, although she was ready for the day, the day did not seem to be really ready for her. Apart from a need to tidy and clean the flat (top, middle and bottom of the list for every weekend, but rarely achieved) there was not a lot to do. She could loiter in Café Franck while Patrice worked, but that seemed a little unimaginative. She could phone around and see if anyone was wanting a visit, but that was hardly likely. Most of her Brussels friends were in couples. There was her Finnish colleague at the European Parliament, Mariana, but she was so intense she was more than likely to prefer spending her Sundays reading Schopenhauer behind closed curtains than pootling around with Catrina.

'If in doubt, procrastinate', thought Catrina, and made herself more tea – backed up this time with toast and Marmite, a breakfast she dared not have in Patrice's presence without bringing down a stream of anti-British culinary derision on her head.

Feeling suitably rebellious she had an extra slice. Guilt soon set in as she put the offending jar of salted brewer's waste back, all the way back, into the cupboard above the sink. And with guilt came the need for expiation. She looked at the weekend's mess of grimy plates and sediment-encrusted mugs and sighed. Cleaning the kitchen had better be the morning's activity. It was as dreary as the weather, and just as inevitable.

She had just finished the plates, knives, spoons and assorted implements, and was refilling the sink with mugs when she heard the chirrup of her mobile phone from somewhere near the bed.

Where, though? She looked first in desperation at her soapy hands, then round the kitchen for a towel, gave up, wiped herself half dry on her jeans and launched into the phone-search operation.

It was not in her bag, and there was no sign of it in the bed, caught in the duvet or the pillows, but it rang still from an impenetrable hiding place. Catrina grew frantic and swore.

The ringing stopped. Now, though, she was just cross. Phones cannot be ghosts. She searched her clothes and clothes drawers, even though the ring had come from the bed. She searched the bed again, lifted the pillows and the mattress. Nothing. She peered underneath. Nothing there except her trainers, still wet from the previous night melted snow. She pulled them out to dry on top of the radiator, and as she upended them, out tumbled the mobile, landing with a thud on to the rug – not the feared crash on to the hard wooden floor.

Its owner swore again and looked at the missed call number. Not one she recognised, but at least not international. She dialled, and after two rings it was answered.

'Hi Catrina.'

'Hi… um, sorry, who have I rung?'

'Mariana. Didn't you recognise my voice?'

'Stupid of me, I know, but I'm afraid not,' said Catrina.

'Are you doing anything? I mean now?'

'Well, not really. Washing up.'

'Up?' Mariana asked.

'The mugs and things.'

'Nothing important, then.'

'It is if you live here.'

'Of course.' Mariana paused. She always found talking to Catrina difficult. She never knew whether the Englishwoman was trying to be funny or not. 'Perhaps we could meet when you have finished.'

If Mariana had been in the room she would have seen Catrina shrug. 'OK. Any particular reason? I mean, we'll probably see each other in Parliament tomorrow. Did you have a good New Year, by the way?'

'Yes – you see, that's why I wanted to meet. I had a great New Year, and I think I have a new boyfriend.'

'And?' Catrina was still baffled as to why Mariana thought this necessitated a meeting. It wasn't as if they even liked each other very much.

'He's English. I don't perhaps understand him so well sometimes. I thought if you could meet him you could tell – am I being foolish?'

'I probably could,' admitted Catrina, 'but would it make a difference? After all, he's going to be your boyfriend, not mine.'

'Please?'

It was a very un-Finnish request, Catrina realised. 'If you really want me to, sure. When?'

'Could you come over to Flagey? Perhaps after twelve-thirty?'

'All right. Patrice is working there anyway, so he can give his opinion too.'

'Will that help?'

Catrina wasn't sure, but the opinion was likely to be given whether or not it helped. She rang off and went back to the sink. Now the day had purpose. She would even have to hurry.

Her telephone rang again. It was Mercedes, her Spanish best friend, with exactly the same request.

First with the News

There was a smile of anticipation and an element of relief as Guus van de Looy ('Fidel' to everybody except his cable TV audience) settled into his usual place by the radiator and window in Café Franck.

He lined up his coffee and his small dark beer and refolded the Sunday newspaper into his preferred format – halved lengthwise and then folded across in a way directly opposite to that intended by its publisher. Fidel was alone and settled in his routine and, had he bothered to realise the fact, was happy. At the very least he felt untroubled. Elise, his younger girlfriend, was spending the first couple of weeks of the new year skiing in the Dolomites with her brother.

Skiing was not Fidel's idea of fun. Although his stringy fifty-something figure didn't show it, exercise of any description was not an activity that he sought. He was happy enough to sit back and admire Elise's lithe and supple frame demonstrating some of the moves she had observed in her Modern Circus Studies. That was his excuse, anyway – and when she had suggested that he go with her to the Italian snow Fidel had demurred, arguing that he was bound to slip on icy pavements on his way back from a day on hot spiced wine.

In truth his real reasons were more complicated. He was fairly certain Elise's brother disapproved of her new relationship, and even Fidel himself was anxious. Thirty years separated them, yet their first three months as neighbours and lovers had passed tests of friction and disagreement without ever being badly threatened. Take them out of their daily lives, living in flats one above the other up the hill from Flagey, though, and Fidel was nervous that the cracks might begin to show. So he had refused the kind invitation, citing pressures of work, and had settled back into his bachelor ways.

As an excuse it was pretty feeble. He hadn't been in to his department at the university since storming out of a lecture many weeks before the end of the previous term. He had announced his resignation publicly, but neither the authorities nor his students seemed to have noticed.

Admittedly they could be forgiven. He had pottered into his office occasionally to pick up books and periodicals. He had carried on supervising his masters students by email and Skype; essays had been marked and returned, reading lists updated. During the months of his absence two lengthy articles on urban social disintegration had appeared in worthy journals, one of them based in Paris and famous enough to set the tight world of French academia chattering. Fidel had found himself on mainstream political shows for both radio and television, not just his weekly hour of cable obscurity. His failure to turn up for staff meetings was greeted with quiet relief by colleagues, who tended to smirk and put it down to his late discovery of his libido.

In Fidel's mind his resignation was a fact. In everybody else's mind he was just off campus and out of their hair for a while.

Quarter of an hour later he had finished and replaced the first of his black coffees – three was the morning's quota before he allowed himself to switch fully to beer or to contemplate anything more intellectually taxing than the newspaper.

Outside the window the Sunday market was in full swing in Flagey's paved square. At eleven o'clock the music was turned up a notch and the early families, desperate for distractions for children in pushchairs, were supplemented by genuine food shoppers and ambling couples not deterred by the January chill or the driving sleet.

Fidel ignored it, as he always did, and returned to his newspaper. The sport, travel, business, arts and lifestyle sections were all extracted and placed under his chair. The last two would be glanced at later, just in case there were events and trends he would have to be aware of when asked for comments. There was a fine line between having a reputation as a crusty commentator and being out of touch. But about sport, business and trawling through winter advice for summer beaches, he cared nothing whatever.

The books pages were read intently and gave the most pleasure – especially those pieces where fellow academics were elegantly demolished. Fidel himself had never written a book, but he had participated in many demolitions. There were two in this edition of the paper, finally appearing after sitting on the editor's desk since October. Their author could barely remember writing them, but he grinned as he reread his own scalpel-sharp wit (as he hoped the world would think of it).

He would have been horrified if he had been told he was an egotistical old bitch – and even more horrified if a critic had lambasted him in the same way (maybe that was secretly why he had never published anything longer than an essay) – but Fidel loved to turn a sharp phrase, and he read his pieces again, sipping his beer with renewed satisfaction and feeling that he could abandon coffee early as a reward. Now that the reviews were published the fees would be in soon; nothing startling, but for a combined total of over a thousand words in Belgium's main Sunday newspaper, nothing to be sniffed at either. Perhaps even another beer did not do the occasion justice. Maybe he might risk a *vin mousseux*. Or two.

It was only when he was finishing the second review for the third time that he noticed the asterisk above the last word and the italicised note from the sub-editor below.

*See News, page 6.

Fidel was baffled, but followed the instruction.

He searched page six, trying to find an article that could possibly be relevant to his review of a book with the deeply un-newsworthy title *Some Reflections on Proto-reactionary Tendencies in Closed Urban Minorities*.

Nothing looked very promising. There were items on constitutional-reform proposals (a regular that never seemed to actually go anywhere), metro trains prone to breakdowns (of which the same was said) and a call for Belgium to contribute more to international peace-keeping operations. Fidel wondered if this was it and the asterisk note had been a joke – an editor's comment on his reviewing style. Then he spotted his own name in a paragraph-long piece far down the furthest column on the right.

It was headlined 'New College Breaks Fee Barriers', and read:

> Moves are far advanced to offer students an alternative to fee-paying or state-run education. Using all the facilities of the Internet, the Collegium Gratis Brusseliensis (CGB) will support itself by advertising, sponsorship and subscriptions to its publications – however, enrolled students worldwide will pay nothing. In a controversial move, likely to cause protests in the German community, students will be able to submit work in French, Flemish or English. Several well-known figures are understood to be considering resigning their conventional academic jobs to join the new college, among them Guus van de Looy, who is also an occasional contributor to this journal – see page 47.

Fidel read the paragraph with mounting alarm.

Change of Direction

Sitting immediately behind Fidel in Café Franck, Flamand was hiding – not from Fidel (whom he did not know) but from his girlfriend Agnestina. Former girlfriend – he really must start thinking of her as that. He must put her firmly behind him, consign her to his autobiography, a paragraph or two to explain the turmoil of his first term at university and the intensity of the poems written in the few weeks of their whirlwind affair.

Flamand could pinpoint exactly the moment he had fallen out of love. It had been when Agnestina had blamed him for not being on time in this very café when he had not only been there but had been early. The café's CCTV system had proved that he had bent down to pick up a pencil at the crucial moment and been slightly hidden from view by a large woman a moment later. Agnestina had not bothered to wait and check again, to linger for a few seconds, even, and, when the issue had been settled in Flamand's favour by the bar staff the next day, had continued to act as if it had been his fault. Flamand had been civil, of course, but as his obsession evaporated, so did his need to see her.

To all of this Agnestina was oblivious, and now, sitting at a table at the other extremity of the L-shaped bar, was equally ignorant of Flamand hiding around the corner. To say she had not noticed his desertion in the last weeks of term would not be quite true. There had been moments when she had wondered at the lack of texts and voicemails, surprised that there had been no invitations, but she had put that down to the pressure of end-of-term essays that were overwhelming her too. Then everyone had dispersed for Christmas – in her case to the family in Mons – and only now were her friends drifting back to Brussels, ready for university life to start again.

Flamand finished his coffee, used the torn biscuit wrapper to mark the place in his book and went to the bar for a refill. Patrice, serving at the other end of the bar, spotted Flamand as he waited for an espresso to filter through, and waved him around. Flamand shook his head and stayed where he was.

'You don't like that end?' asked Patrice, when he had eventually finished serving his more conveniently placed customer and found a suitable occasion to venture north.

'That end is fine,' admitted Flamand, 'but perhaps this morning I prefer to—'

'Wait alone?' completed Patrice, with half a flash of inspiration. 'What will you have – *café au lait*, as usual?'

'No, my usual has changed. Black and double, please.'

'If you say so,' shrugged Patrice, wondering what had happened to the young man over the Christmas break. Perhaps he had just grown up. Certainly his taste in coffee had.

He brought back the fresh cupful and, as Flamand handed over two euros, said, 'Your girlfriend is in here this morning too, you know.'

'I know,' said Flamand, without peering round to find her. 'Former girlfriend.'

'Ah!' said Patrice, closing the subject like all good barmen and moving on to the next customer. A few minutes later he had the time to glance in the other direction, over to Agnestina, intent on her computer in the far corner by the window, nearest the entrance to the concert hall. She really was lovely, thought, Patrice. That shade of hair which made it hard to tell if she was a blonde on the edge of being a redhead or a brown so light that it was impossible to decide which of the three colours dominated at any moment. He could hardly fail to notice her cascading long hair because she rarely left it alone, twirling and fiddling, tying it behind, piling it on top of her head then letting it fall down her back again.

She had clearly dumped her young admirer, Patrice assured himself. Her self-assurance, her poise, her absorption, her gorgeousness made the alternative too absurd to contemplate. Flamand was simply not in her class.

As though she had intercepted his thoughts, Agnestina looked up and caught Patrice looking at her. She held his gaze without expression for a moment before letting the briefest and slightest of smiles play at the side of her lips. Patrice gave her an equally tiny nod of recognition in return before returning to his duties with brisk efficiency.

Agnestina thought about their exchange for a second, looked back at her computer screen and the page of Facebook titbits she had been scrolling through, then clicked it to the screensaver and strolled over to the bar.

She was third in the queue, but Patrice was expert in taking several orders at once if it suited him, so there was hardly a pause between her reaching the counter and his acknowledgement. 'Mademoiselle?'

'Hallo.'

Patrice nodded, then carried on with his work at the coffee geyser, giving her an occasional look over his shoulder in case she wished to give him her decision about drinks.

She didn't.

The queue was served and Patrice was free to face her. 'It is nice to see you again. Did you have a good New Year?'

'Yes, I think so,' she said. 'And you?'

'Nothing special but, you know… it was OK.'

'You have a girlfriend?' she asked suddenly.

Patrice smiled. 'Yes, I think so. Why?'

'I thought you would be too busy.'

'I am never too busy for a beautiful woman, mademoiselle, but it is true that at the moment one in particular occupies most of the time when I am not serving here.'

'I see.'

'And you have a friend too, I seem to remember?' he asked.

'I thought so. I am not so sure now. He has lost interest, I think.'

'Really? I find that hard to believe.' Patrice's gallantry was turned up to maximum and, since Agnestina had still failed to give him an order he took matters in hand and gave her a glass of *vin mousseux*. Agnestina was surprised but gratified.

'For me?'

'Of course – for a happy New Year.'

'Thank you.'

'I don't think you ever told me your name. I am Patrice.'

'Agnestina.'

It was at that moment that Mercedes bustled into the room, followed closely by Catrina.

Being Metaphorical

In Esko Nystrom's apartment across the lake from Flagey, the actress Amelie Poitiers was in the throes of an unexpectedly tearful goodbye. She was parting from her Member of the European Parliament for the first time in nearly two weeks, and she found herself blubbing like a schoolgirl in love with the art master at the end of term. There was no particular reason to be upset. She had a film to make, but this involved spending two months in the south of France around Cap Ferrat, and Esko had agreed that there was no very good reason why he should not join her there for a long weekend in ten days' time.

But in fact, there was a very good reason why escaping to the Riviera at the first opportunity in the New Year with his film-star lover might be not quite so clever for Esko. He had just been elected leader of his political group in Parliament, and such a jaunt might seem too like the antics of his flamboyant Italian predecessor to be to his colleagues' liking. They had, after all, elected him to bring a touch of austere Finnish Lutheranism to the role – at least, in theory. While an appropriate degree of gravitas and dependability was hoped for, there was also the realisation that getting their small group of thirty Social, Liberal, Enterprise and Ecology (SLEE) members talked about in the general press of Europe was an uphill task. So just a touch of stardust was no bad thing. Not too often on the Riviera, though, and no sunbathing with (or in) magnums of champagne.

Amelie had pointed out that even on the Riviera nobody was stupid enough to try to sunbathe in early January. Esko's reply – that as a Frenchwoman she should know that he was being metaphorical – earned him his first display of actress temperament.

Theirs had been a whirlwind romance in the best traditions of the genre. They had met in October at a film-festival screening across in the Flagey Centre where, at the reception which followed, she was the guest of honour and he had failed to recognise her after watching her act on film for two hours. Within three days they had found that the press had declared them an item and, rather to their own surprise, they had agreed.

Since then reality had taken over. Amelie had been busy until close to Christmas promoting her latest film. Esko had been dealing with the political fallout from the ousting of Roberto Vincenzi after charges of corruption had surfaced in Italy – charges that Vincenzi refuted to the extent that he had done nothing the rest of Tuscany's public servants weren't doing – using his expenses other than for the strictly authorised purpose. This had cut little ice with the puritanical Germans, and Esko had been shoved into Vincenzi's place, almost whether he liked it or not. Meanwhile, at home in Finland his wife Rikka was cementing their estrangement by equally publicly toying with a tenor from the Helsinki Opera. (Esko was starting to realise every thought of her was prefaced by the word 'meanwhile'.)

He had returned to Helsinki for the Christmas break to find himself portrayed there as the poor cuckold. His parents were embarrassed, his friends sympathetic. Esko's relaxed response — that it was probably all for the best and that anyway, he was too busy with new interests in his life to worry about it — was treated as commendable but unbelievable martyrdom; just what they would expect, but a repression that would cause trouble later in his forties. After all, he had been so in love with Rikka for years!

Rikka, though, was now intent on a domestic political career and local celebrity which made Esko an irrelevance. Worse — once he had been made leader of his party in Brussels he was competition! What if he came home and moved seriously into the national arena? For Rikka, who assumed, like all those who love power, that everybody was as ambitious as she was, the prospect was intolerable. When Esko had tried to tell her, over a last drink in what had been their shared flat in Helsinki's most newly fashionable district, that his acquisition by Amelie made this less, not more, likely, she simply didn't believe him. It was all a plot to thwart her.

Esko had returned to Brussels before New Year exhausted. When Amelie announced that she had had just as much of her parents and cousins in Paris as she could stand, the solution was clear. They would hole up together at Flagey until work resumed. It was, after all, where no one would expect them to be. Brussels — at least the Brussels of the European institutions — should be deserted, and all good French movie actors should be on the beaches of Martinique or Guadalupe.

They had been untroubled. They had read a lot, slept a lot, made love a lot.

Now real life was cutting in, and Amelie wanted real life to go away. With two suitcases by her side and a taxi waiting outside in the driving sleet, Amelie sobbed into Esko's shoulder as he kissed her neck and hair.

Eventually he murmured, 'I suppose you should go, or you'll miss the plane.'

She shrugged. 'So what? There's another one in an hour or two.'

'Then you will be late arriving and people will be angry.'

'Let them be.'

Esko admitted to himself that she had a point. After all, what was the point in being a star if you couldn't be unreliable? Two days late would be a problem, two hours barely even noticeable. 'Fine,' he said. 'Let's get the ticket changed and you can go this afternoon, after some lunch.'

Esko was being reasonable. It was the only thing Amelie hated about him. She burrowed deeper into his shoulder. There was a long pause.

'Do you want to do that?'

Amelie mumbled.

'Is that a yes?' Esko whispered.

'No.'

He was flummoxed. 'So…?'

'If I don't go now I won't go at all. There is no point postponing this till later.'

'One more kiss, then we'll go.'

She obliged. At length Esko prised her away and began to carry the suitcases out of the apartment and down the stairs. 'Do you want me to come to the airport with you?'

'No, absolutely not.'

'You're sure?' he asked.

'Yes… I mean no… Could you?'

'Of course.'

He dumped the cases at the bottom of the stairs and went back for his coat. So they had lunch together anyway, with Amelie amazed to find that they were shown without even asking into the VIP area because the airline check-in man had seen her latest film only the night before and had fallen in love with her even faster than Esko had managed.

Dismissing Nations

Mercedes and Catrina were almost in step as they entered the café together and, beaming, strode to the bar where Patrice was just finishing handing Agnestina a glass of bubbly white wine. Neither of them gave the student so much as a glance.

'You look happy,' remarked Patrice, tearing his eyes away from Agnestina's retreating figure.

'Why wouldn't we be?' asked Catrina.

'Of course you should be. But it is cold outside and you have just walked from nice warm apartments.'

'If you think back five hours you'll remember that my flat is neither warm nor nice,' Catrina pointed out.

Her lover considered saying something gallant, but in the end just shrugged and asked, 'Coffee?' He had already turned to start the process before there was an answer.

'I'd better look for a table,' said Catrina. 'It's fuller than I expected. I'm not sure it's going to be easy to find one for three of us.' She moved off and began to survey the room. There was an unattractive table for two in a distant corner, masked from the outside world by a curtain. Catrina went for it and bagged an extra chair from nearby. She sat with her back to the door and main area of the room, feeling that Mercedes would need to spot her new boyfriend and then seat him close.

Patrice carried on with his train of thought as he laid out the tray and loaded the coffee saucers with spoon, sugar and biscuits. 'So you have good news?'

'Nothing really,' said Mercedes, still smiling so hard it made the statement absurd. 'I think I may have a new man in my life, that's all.'

This time Patrice's gallant side was up to the task. 'In which case, that is news indeed. Congratulations. Will we meet him?'

'I hope – at least, he should be here very soon. That is why I wanted Catrina to be here. I want to know what she thinks.'

'Oh?' Patrice looked mildly puzzled. He knew Catrina and Mercedes had become firm friends, but he was surprised Mercedes needed her to vet her acquisition so early in the year.

'He's English, you see. From Scotland,' she said, thus committing a worse gaffe than calling a Catalan Spanish.

'So!' That explained the matter.

Catalan Mercedes was not sure if she was reading the new man in her life right – whether his interest was genuine or whether he was just pretending to like her by adopting that infuriating false intimacy that young Englishmen used to counter their reputation for cold aloofness.

Patrice became conspiratorial. 'Soon you and I will need to compare notes. We must see if having an English woman and an English man as a lover have similarities.'

'We shall,' smiled Mercedes, 'but perhaps not just yet.' Patrice bowed as he placed the full coffee cups on a tray and Mercedes carried it over to the table.

The matter was forgotten as an influx of churchgoers, their Sunday suits and stern dresses at complete odds with the jeans and fleeces of the relaxed and less religious regulars, filed up to the bar and kept Patrice busy at the coffee machine.

The question Catrina put to Mercedes after they had licked the first of the coffee froth from their lips was almost the same as Patrice's. 'What's he like, then – and does he have a name?'

Mercedes grinned slyly. 'I don't think I want to tell you – you must make up your own mind. He should be here in a minute.'

'All right, but in that case, where did you meet him? Did he come into the gallery? Does he come to the *vernissage* evenings? Have I seen him there already?' In fact Catrina had only been to two *vernissages* – the same two at which Mercedes herself had been on hand since starting as assistant in Nikita's gallery a little way up the hill towards Avenue Louise from Flagey.

'No – at least, not as far as I know. I'm not even sure he likes art.'

That was black mark number one in Catrina's book. She was no great expert herself, but she knew contemporary art was becoming central to Mercedes' world, and couldn't see a relationship lasting in which the boyfriend stood around private views looking bored at best, sneering at worst (which was likely, given that Nikita had a thing for artists who were nothing if not challenging).

'I met him shopping.'

'Shopping?'

'Yes – is that surprising?'

'Well, I suppose not. I mean… What sort of shopping? Was he looking for shoes, or buying loo paper, or stalking around the girls' underclothes floors in Printemps?'

'No! Catrina, you're not being fair. He was choosing chocolates in the Place Sablon. He asked me which I thought were the best.'

'Why?'

'Why – I don't know. Because I was there?'

'Because you are pretty and he wanted to chat you up, more like.'

Mercedes was tiring of the English woman's cynicism. 'Why shouldn't he?'

'Sorry.' Catrina realised she had gone too far. She was projecting her own wariness on to her friend, and anyway, her meeting with Patrice would never have happened if her own clumsiness had not covered Mercedes in mint tea, so she could hardly complain about accidental meetings. Not everything in life came about through formal introductions that would have seemed suitably decorous to Jane Austen. She took a gulp of coffee, nibbled the sweet biscuit and said, 'I just hope he wasn't targeting you, I suppose.'

'Maybe I made sure he did,' confessed Mercedes. 'He's very handsome, and I'm so bored with Spanish boys.'

'Oh, so he's not Spanish?'

'Not even Latin. Very northern, in fact.'

'Is that why you want my opinion so badly?'

'It could be.'

Catrina paused and looked into her empty cup. 'I'm really not the best person to ask, you know. I mean, if he's German I'm prejudiced, if he's Danish or Swedish he'll bore me to death. I've no time for the Poles, the Dutch or the Lithuanians.'

'British?'

'God no! Though I suppose the Welsh can be all right,' she conceded, 'and the occasional Scot.'

'So that leaves me a man from Finland…'

'Not Esko, surely?'

'Don't be silly… Estonia, Latvia, Flanders or Ireland.'

'You could try an Icelander or a Norwegian.'

'Not in the EU,' Mercedes pointed out. They were both laughing now.

'I'll get us more coffee.' Catrina stood up and carried the empties back to the bar. Patrice had disappeared for moment into the back room, so she ordered from his colleague Damien without involving herself in any conversation.

As usual Damien was dealing with five orders at once, so a few minutes passed before Catrina was able to pick up the refills and turn back to her seat. Concentrating hard on not spilling (there was history, after all), she was almost at the table when she realised there was already someone new sitting with Mercedes. And not just anyone.

Catrina froze. 'Shit. Bruno,' she said out loud, but not loud enough for her ex- and very despised boyfriend, the thick Tory spiv, to hear. She stood still for a moment, wondering what to do. Mercedes was too busy watching Bruno to notice.

Catrina turned, put the full cups of coffee back on the chrome counter and fled out into the freezing afternoon.

Air Time

Luckily for Elise her hangover did not seem to be impairing her ability to snowboard. This thought occurred to her as she hurtled down one of the more startling slopes above the Italian village of Moena in the Val di Fassa.

It was also the last thought she had before the spike of a concealed rock sent her board one way and gravity sent her another.

The feeling of free flight was something her researches in Modern Circus Studies had thrown up as one of the most exhilarating available to trapeze artists, especially those in the new circuses that combined extreme elements of drama and dance with more traditional acrobatics. Studies had not prepared her, though, for the sensation of somersaulting in the clear air of the Dolomites, of seeing the ground down which she had been boarding appear first behind and then above her, nor for the out-of-body experience of watching herself as if on film being reunited with the snow and the ground underneath a hundred metres away from where she had launched.

That was interesting, her brain told her as Elise lay prone in the snow, which seemed relatively soft – relatively meaning that it was softer than the layer of ice a few centimetres underneath.

SUNDAY

She stared at the sky for a few seconds.

She wondered vaguely how she was going to get to the bottom of the mountain without a snowboard. Slithering down on her backside was going to be undignified and cold. Walking was a pastime the slope made impossible. Elise raised herself on to her elbows and surveyed the scene: magnificent, beautiful, forbidding – and deserted.

She looked down to where the village nestled like a cartoon creation; an unreal and distant prospect. Then she saw that her foot was pointing in the opposite direction from her knee and passed out.

When she came to she was aware of a faint swishing and a lovely feeling of being carried through the air with no effort from her own body. Maybe I've been picked up by an eagle, she dreamt, and he's flying me to his lair in the highest of the mountains, away from all the ski lifts and tourists. I shall be an egret. She tried to raise her arm to greet him, but she couldn't move. Her arms, indeed all parts of her, were strapped firmly.

Tentatively Elise opened her eyes. The sky was cloudlessly blue and she could sense the sun above the mountains on the other side of the valley. Closer, much closer, she saw the back of a man dressed in red who seemed to be steering her. She was tied to a sledge, she realised, inside a bag which seemed just like the sleeping bag she used for camping. That was when the pain hit and her brain, sensibly deciding that the next few moments were not going to be much fun, switched off again.

The lights above her were soft when she woke, and around her voices murmured in a language she felt she should understand but didn't. At least she could move her arms, though something uncomfortable was sticking into the back of her right hand. There was no helmet on her head any more, but moving seemed to be just as difficult as it had been on the sledge. When was that? She had no idea.

A nurse in white appeared, spoke to her in Italian and went away again. What had she said? Elise was puzzled. Normally she could manage Italian. A man appeared, in grey this time, with a clipboard and forms. He peered at her doubtfully. '*Italiano?*'

Elise tried to shake her head but couldn't. Somehow the muscles were not interested in obeying her brain. '*Non,*' she whispered, thinking she was shouting.

The man in the grey suit bent closer. '*Inglese?*'

'*Non. Français.*' Elise was confusing herself now. She spent a third of her life at least speaking English in Brussels. Not today, though, not now. Other languages would have to wait.

'*Ah! Grazie. Momento, signorina.*' He left and returned with a different nurse who smiled down at her and in French asked her name, age and where she came from. The nurse apologised. Her friends on the mountain had given some of the information to the rescue team, but now it was necessary to check. Was there someone she would like the hospital to call – her parents, maybe?'

'What happened?'

The nurse shrugged. 'You fell. Nothing unusual, but now…'

Gradually the wooziness that had clouded Elise's mind was fading. Shapes were becoming sharper, but calling up the answers to even these simple questions was an effort. She tried to remember her parents' number but couldn't.

'Do you have my phone?'

SUNDAY

The nurse spoke to the man with the clipboard and he relayed the answer. 'We do, but we would prefer you not to call anybody just now.'

Elise was grateful for that. The last thing she wanted to do was to have to explain anything to her parents – or even Fidel. Fidel! They should have his number too. 'I need my phone to give you my parents' number. And my brother's. He is here.'

The nurse reached into the pouch hanging at the side of the trolley bed and tapped on the contacts icon before handing it to Elise. She lifted her right hand to touch the screen and only then noticed the tubes and the tap. Suddenly a shaft of pain struck, as though consciousness had to come at a price. She gave the phone back to the nurse. 'I'm sorry. You do it. My parents are there as Maman. My brother is Artur.' The nurse nodded, found the number and read it to the man in the suit. 'Can you tell me what is wrong with me?'

There was another brief conversation before the nurse replied. 'Signorina, you fell badly. We know you have hurt your left leg. There may be ligament damage to your knee too. As well it is possible that you have broken, or at least cracked, your pelvis. And you are a little concussed – perhaps more than a little. We need you to sign one or two forms so we can take you to X-ray, then possibly to theatre for an operation later, when the swelling is a little better.'

Elise lay quite still, then let the tears come. 'I've never been in hospital,' she said. The resistance of a few minutes earlier evaporated, 'Can I call Fidel?'

'Fidel?'

'Fidel – Guus. My friend.'

The man in the suit shook his head.

'When you have signed these forms,' said the nurse. 'Maybe later. But perhaps it will be easier if I do that.'

A question slowly surfaced. 'Where am I?'

'Bolzano. Ospedale San Antonio.'

A Skirmish

Catrina paused on the pavement outside Flagey – a brave thing to do given the driving sleet. The freezing air began to take the heat out of the panic at seeing her new best friend Mercedes sitting cosily with her new worst acquaintance, Bruno. It was intolerable, but wouldn't it be sensible to at least see what the score between them was? Maybe she could provoke Bruno into saying something so tiresome, so absurd that even Mercedes could see what a creep he was. She could save her friend a lot of pain. She herself had realised the man was a slug after three weeks, but it had taken her more than a month to actually ditch him – an appalling waste of time.

'Hallo,' came a voice from beside her.

Catrina jumped. At first she didn't recognise the muffled figure in black, with only the nose and eyes visible.

'What are you doing out here? I thought only us Finns stood around in this weather!'

'Oh, hi Mariana,' she said. In truth she had completely forgotten that it was Mariana whom she had originally set out to meet, and whose new boyfriend she was meant to assess, not Mercedes'. Running into Mercedes as they arrived in Flagey at the same time had been pure accident. 'I was just going back inside. Patrice came out here for a smoke,' she lied.

'Let's go in, then,' said Mariana reasonably.

Patrice was still in the back room when they arrived at the counter, so Catrina did not have to extend the lie. Nonetheless Damien looked at her quizzically as she returned with Mariana. 'I thought you'd left. I threw the coffees away. Do you want more?'

This should have been a simple question, but for Catrina it was anything but. Should she get two and go to sit with Mariana as far away from Bruno and Mercedes as possible? Should she buy two and go back to Mercedes as she had originally planned, letting Mariana buy her own if necessary, and put up with the inevitable social bile of having to be civil to Bruno? Or should she get four and sit atop the moral high ground by being utterly magnanimous to her ex as a way of marking the new year?

'Well I certainly need coffee, now – black and extra-large,' announced Mariana, tired of waiting for Catrina to answer.

'Double?' asked Damien.

'Triple.'

Furtively, Catrina glanced over her right shoulder to where Mercedes and Bruno had been sitting. She frowned. Mercedes was there, watching her inquiringly, but Bruno was nowhere to be seen. Catrina was even more confused, but summoned up the presence of mind to answer Damien at last. 'Yes, please. Two more cappuccinos, and I'll get Mariana's too.'

'Thanks.'

'Do you know Mercedes?' asked Catrina, as Damien went to get the machine working.

'No, I don't think so,' said Mariana. 'Is she in Parliament too?'

'She thought about it, but not very hard, I don't think. She's more interested in arts than politics. Nikita has given her a job at the gallery up the road. Esko and Amelie know her. They come along to the *vernissage* evenings.'

A month before any mention of Esko and Amelie in the same breath would have sent Mariana's face puckering on the edge of tears, but now she was able just to shrug. 'I won't have been there, then.'

They carried the coffee over to where Mercedes was sitting, resting her arm gratefully against a radiator at the table for three, and introductions were made.

'I thought you'd left me,' said Mercedes.

'No, just joined Patrice for a minute when he wanted a cigarette,' Catrina lied again.

'In this weather?' Mercedes shivered at the thought. 'You're both mad.'

'Could we find a bigger table?' suggested Mariana. 'My boyfriend's coming in a minute. I think there's one free behind you.'

'Sure,' said Mercedes. 'That makes sense, because mine is meant to be here soon too.'

Catrina frowned as they moved across. If Mercedes' boyfriend had not arrived, then that meant he could not be Bruno. Instantly her mood brightened with the relief. Her frown became one of puzzlement rather than concern. Within seconds, though, it had changed back to irritation and disapproval. The expression had not changed at all – she just looked grumpy throughout – but the emotion underlying it would have sent an oscillator wave leaping and plunging.

There was a man standing to her left and his hands were on Mariana's shoulders.

'Hi, Catrina, happy New Year.'

'Hallo, Bruno.'

'I saw you earlier getting coffee but then your friend said you had gone.'

'No, just getting some air.'

'In this weather?'

'What are you doing here, Bruno?'

Mariana spoke up. 'He's meeting me. He's the one I wanted you to meet – but I see that you know each other already.'

'Oh yes,' said Catrina with feeling.

'May I sit down?' asked Bruno with forced politeness.

'Feel free.' Instead of waving Bruno to the seat empty opposite her Catrina stood up and vacated the chair next to Mariana. 'It's all yours.'

Mercedes was watching this English anti-courtship dance with increasing incomprehension. 'I thought...' she began.

'I'm afraid you thought wrong,' Catrina broke in quietly. 'I did know this – this boy, much too well for a few weeks last year. It is something I really regret. Mariana...'

'Now look here,' Bruno protested, 'I was perfectly nice to you. If you couldn't make up your mind about anything or see that what I said was right, that was your problem. Mariana is not having the same difficulties.'

For once Catrina was not to be thwarted. 'Mariana, as I was about to ask, what exactly do you agree with him on? His devotion to Mrs Thatcher's memory? The perfection of big business? How climate change is all make-believe? Or that England will never be great until it shakes off Europe, Scotland and Wales and recolonises America? Oh, and that women should know their place – which is, by the way, arse up to him.'

'Hang on!'

Now that hostilities were out in the open, in good Spanish fashion, Mercedes was much more comfortable. She was immediately on Catrina's side. 'Is any of that true?'

'Well, not put like that it's not!'

'Some of it?'

'Yes, but... Look here, I didn't come here to have a fight. I came here to have a nice Sunday lunchtime with Mariana.'

'How quaint,' rebuffed Catrina. 'Mariana, let's talk about this later. Call me this evening if you're alone. Mercedes, shall we?' Mercedes raised an eyebrow. 'Move,' Catrina spelt it out.

They moved, but Mercedes, who had only just met Mariana, was disturbed to see what Catrina was too indignant to notice – that the Finnish woman was crying.

II

Sunday Carried On

Cold Wine for a Cold Sunday

Saskia van Katwijk was bored. She was always bored on Sundays. At twenty-eight she was not a woman who had hobbies, who went to church – which in her case, if she followed family tradition from the Hague, would have been a sect of Dutch Anabaptists emphatically not available in Catholic Brussels – or who had, at the moment, lovers. She had experimented with one of her own gender in the autumn and, while being an experiment worth one weekend, she found thereafter that going to bed with a woman was just as boring as going to bed with a man. The problem was simple enough. After all the sexual exercise and moderate pleasure they all wanted to talk – about their feelings, their futures, their stories. Basically Saskia had discovered she couldn't care less.

That, surely, did not have to be so complicated. At work, where she was the second assistant to a Netherlands centre-right Member of the European Parliament, she turned up, processed papers which meant nothing to her, ensured her Member was where he was meant to be, or, in silence, took notes at meetings for him, and then went home. She had a routine which involved cycling to work like all Dutch women should, even in the unnecessary hills of Brussels (another complication – untidy landscape explained untidy religion), not a moment after seven-thirty in the morning, then taking a run around Parc Leopold for forty-five minutes exactly. She would shower in the facilities provided for staff in the offices and be at her desk with a sugar-free black coffee by nine o'clock on the dot. If nobody had come into the office by nine-thirty – an example of the world's laxity but none of her business – she would walk briskly down to the Mickey Mouse Parliament bar and have another coffee, watching all the tired early morning expressions of her colleagues with disdain.

In the evenings Saskia would visit the gym for an hour, follow it with good steak and frites, which was just about the only thing she was prepared to accept Brussels did better than Holland, and wash it down with two large glasses of dry, very dry, white wine. That, and hours of gaming and an online-chat persona utterly different from her reality, suited Saskia very well, thank you.

Nevertheless, Sundays bored her.

The beginnings and ends could be adapted easily enough – a little later out of bed, a run around a different park, a longer shower, an hour or two extra online – but the day in the middle was excruciating. Saskia had no obsessions or diversions. Unlike Mariana she had no attachment to worthy causes or hankering after the depths of philosophers and poets. Music was just so much noise. Museums bored her even more than being bored.

She could have enjoyed sport but, while she cared about winning, she did not have enough of a stake in competition to make her try hard. If she had no interest in other people it really didn't matter if they won or not, as long as Saskia had achieved a personal best. After a while even that lost its fascination.

This Sunday was worse than ever. She had returned from the Christmas and New Year break the night before: a pleasant time with her parents who had been as unexacting towards her as she could have wished. Her father (a civil servant in the Ministry of Waterways) and her mother (a police woman close to retirement) were genuinely proud of their daughter's choice of career. They would have preferred her to be thinking of providing grandchildren, but were aware that these days there was no point in mentioning the issue until she was over thirty.

At about the same time as Mercedes and Catrina (whose friendship had started thanks to Saskia's off-handedness) were confronting Bruno, Saskia was staring at the sleet streaking her window and scowling as if that alone would frighten the weather into better behaviour. It worked with most people she encountered. The Brussels winter was used to such scowls, however, and ignored her.

She considered going back to her online netherworld, or perhaps even trying to find a half-watchable film, but even that held no charm. By now she was feeling thoroughly sorry for herself. For Saskia, though, sorrow did not come in parcels of depression but of supercilious resentment at the rest of humanity for failing to entertain her. Revenge was the way to happiness; hard to exact revenge on a wet January afternoon at home in her own flat. She strode across to the quarter of the room reserved as a kitchen and opened the fridge, looking for her usual bottle of Orvieto. There was none. She growled in frustration, a scarring contralto growl like parts of an engine disintegrating that, had anyone been there to hear it, would have had them fleeing to the hills.

In fury she pushed her arms into her black anorak, tugged a woolly hat from the pocket and headed down the two flights of stairs to the street – a narrow one of dour buildings leading at an angle uphill off Rue Malibran, that dingy thoroughfare so unfairly named after one of the greatest singers of all time.

It was an irony of contemporary life that in Rue Malibran there were plenty of Moroccan convenience stores with a good selection of cheap wines for a Sunday drinker. Saskia was a regular visitor to the one on her corner – yet, such was her nature and her disinterest in contact, neither she nor Ahmet (who served her most days and many nights) ever gave any suggestion in their expressions that they had seen each other before. She selected two ready-chilled (barely necessary – she could have left them on her windowsill and achieved the same effect in ten minutes) bottles of Orvieto, and a monster bag of pistachio nuts, and hurried back to her antiseptic home.

Once settled on the sofa with wine and nuts Saskia realised she was little better off than before except that she had the chance to be both drunk and bored. Beside the wine glass on the side table was the pad of blank paper and the pen she used for making lists. For want of anything better to do she picked them up, slugged down some white wine and began to draw. It was something she had not done since schooldays, when doodling in the margins of her exercise books was the only way to deal with the eternity of lessons.

After a while a face emerged from the aggressive random strokes: a silly vacuous face with frenetic hair. Saskia looked at in surprise, as though meeting someone she knew in a tram. To the face she added a bulbous body and tiny legs. A bubble sprouted from the mouth and Saskia added words that were acidic and scatological.

For the first time all day the Dutchwoman grinned. Caricaturist. She had found a new vocation.

Impossible News

When the call rang through to Fidel as he lay on his sofa reading more of the papers on that January Sunday afternoon, he thought at first it was a wrong number, then a joke.

'Signor Fidel?' asked the voice at the other end, deep but female.

Fidel thought about it. The greeting was all wrong. If it had been a friend the number would not have read 'unknown' and she would not have addressed him as Signor. If it was not a friend, she would have asked for Monsieur van de Looy, and not in Italian, but if she was not a friend, how would she have his number – unless she was a bank, and his bank most certainly did not work on Sunday.

'*Oui?*' was, however, all he answered.

'Ah, signor, forgive me. Your friend, Signorina Elise, has asked me to call you especially.'

'Who are you?' asked Fidel, not unreasonably.

'Forgive me again, signor. This is the Ospedale San Antonio in Bolzano. La signorina was brought here after her accident.'

Fidel sat up straight and immediately felt sick. 'What accident?'

'Apparently she fell while snowboarding. It is not uncommon in the mountains, but unfortunately on this occasion—'

'Is she all right?'

'Signor, it depends how you define "all right". She is alive and resting. However—'

'In danger?'

'Sì, there was a moment – indeed perhaps an hour or two—'

The mounting panic in Fidel was beginning to make him breathe unevenly, but he managed to blurt out, 'Please, how is she? Please tell me!'

The nurse had the Italian tendency of giving all the extraneous detail first before coming to the nub of the matter. 'The doctor says that in the circumstances, given the need to operate, and the clear concussion she suffered when she landed, and the fact that she was unconscious even when her friends had raised the alarm, and though the rescuers were able to reach her remarkably quickly given the busy time of day… Thankfully the weather has been fine and indeed much better than all this week…'

'Please…' Fidel's entreaty was almost pathetic.

'Sì, signor, sì. She is under sedation. She has some little broken bones, and we are concerned there may be others, maybe some important ones. Her head will need to recover gently too. But she will be OK, we think. Perhaps not this week, though.'

The relief flowed through Fidel as the nurse's reassurance, partial though it was, sank in. 'Should I be there?'

The nurse sounded surprised that he had even asked. 'I do not know what your relationship is with Signorina Elise, signor. Hospital policy is that only family and, er, partners may visit at this stage, but since you are in Belgium and it will, no doubt, take some time for you to reach Bolzano, I think perhaps tomorrow morning or a little later la signorina would appreciate it, as she asked me particularly to telephone you, signor.'

'I see. Yes, of course. I must come.'

'I think that is wise.'

'Please tell Elise I will see her tomorrow. The hospital of St Anthony, you said?'

'That is correct and I will tell her. Goodbye.'

The phone went dead despite the list of questions Fidel had begun to formulate only at the end of the call. He stared helplessly at the silent object in his hands and wondered what on earth to do next. Book a train or a plane, of course – but it was a Sunday afternoon, and despite his trendy TV image, Fidel was not king of the Internet. He did not trawl through interactive websites or have an account with an online system. He would, on the rare occasions that he needed to stray beyond the Belgian border, just wander over to the booking office at the Gare du Midi or, if he wanted to go by air, into the travel agent a few doors down from his apartment, which these days only dealt in holidays but was prepared to book him a ticket if he looked pathetic enough.

How did one get from Brussels to Bolzano, anyway? Did it even have an airport? If not, how would he know where to fly to and get the train onwards – Milan, Venice? He had no idea. He could try French Google, he supposed. Suddenly, though, a fresh wave of panic hit him, together with delayed reaction to the news that Elise was injured and in danger. Fidel was not Action Man but needed to act, and yet all he could do was slump on to the sofa and shake. After a few minutes he knew he needed three things: someone to talk to, help with getting to Bolzano and a drink.

He gathered his coat, gloves, scarf and hat, found the waterproof case for his laptop and then thought it would be useless so put it away again before heading out of the flat. He passed Elise's door and wondered whether he should go in, whether there was anything he should take her. How long would she have to stay in Bolzano? How would she get home? And when she did, how would she make it up the stairs? The questions were crowding him again.

Out on the street the sleet still fell, pretending it was lighter than rain but finding its way into crevices in clothing that rain would not have penetrated. Fidel walked as fast as was safe down the hill to Flagey, head bent low and hat gripped firmly against the wind. He had no real idea why he was going to the Café Franck. If he had thought about it, the answer would have been that it was a place of safety in his psyche and one populated enough for there to be an acquaintance to hand, even on a Sunday afternoon. Elise worked there, after all. If nothing else the men behind the bar should be told. Heaven knew when she would be able to do a shift again.

Meanwhile Esko had returned from the airport, where he had been seeing Amelie safely into the VIP lounge on her way to Nice. He couldn't face going straight back into his empty flat on the other side of the lake, so he made the taxi driver drop him off in front of the Arts Centre. He and Fidel arrived at the entrance to the café together.

News Spreads

The door of Café Franck was held open for Esko and Fidel by Catrina, who was trying to make an indignant and pointed exit after her brush with her detested ex-boyfriend, Bruno. She wanted to force her way out, plainly fuming, head held high against the prevailing winter. Instead she found herself holding the door.

'Oh, hallo,' she said, recognising both but not sure if they knew each other.

It was Esko who answered first. 'Happy New Year. Thanks, Catrina.'

'Thanks, and to you.' She switched to French. 'Bonjour, Fidel. How's Elise?'

'It's a disaster. I don't know what to do. They are operating on her now.'

Both Catrina and Esko were brought up short. Esko had been pausing inside the door just long enough to be polite because he had no idea who Fidel was. Catrina had already been edging her way out.

'Operating? What's happened?' asked Catrina. She closed the door again, shutting out the bitter wind.

'She fell – skiing, I think. One of those sports. This morning, in Italy. She is in a hospital – Bolzano.'

Esko, ever the politician, needed no introduction to a man before asking him a question. 'Is she hurt badly?'

'She must be. I don't know,' Fidel looked at him dully then turned back to Catrina. 'I have to get there, but I don't know how – not today.'

'Awful,' Catrina said helplessly.

She was effectively blocking the door, and was made aware of the fact as it was nudged firmly into her back. Moving to one side to let the newcomer in, she was confronted by a small man in his early thirties with laughing eyes wearing a woolly hat with the legend 'Hearts For Ever' woven into its brim. 'Sorry – *pardonnez-moi*,' he said in a broad Scots accent.

'My fault,' acknowledged Catrina, turning to face him. The Scotsman failed to come any further into the room, however, in his turn holding the door open. 'Oh, I'm not leaving. I was, but…' Catrina tried but failed to explain.

'No, but we are,' announced a sibilant English voice behind her. 'If you'll allow us, that is.'

'Of course,' said the Scotsman, straightening up and immediately certain that, whoever this man was, he disliked him. Catrina stepped to one side without turning her head. She knew Bruno's voice, and she also knew that if she caught his eye he would not be able to resist a parting shot. Bruno left, but Mariana, who was forming what looked like a queue, felt her arm tugged.

'Can I say Happy New Year before I see you in the office tomorrow?' asked Esko.

Mariana had been so wrapped up in the spat between Bruno and Catrina that she had failed to notice her employer. 'Oh, it's you. You're back,' she observed unnecessarily.

'I am. See you tomorrow, then,' Esko said cordially, even though she had walked out of the door after Bruno without continuing the greeting. Bruno had pushed forward, keener to jostle Catrina as he left than to wait for his new friend. The Finnish MEP, though, was too relieved to see that his assistant had a new man in her life to care one way or the other about her lapse of civility. It was, in any case, nothing compared to the alternate storms and ice she had thrown at him in the weeks after he had taken up with Amelie.

Catrina let the door swing shut behind Mariana and Bruno. 'I thought you were leaving too?' said Esko.

'I was, but...' she nodded towards Fidel, who was standing by them but looking round the room wildly as if expecting Elise to emerge suddenly and for the whole nightmare to be over. His hair, blown into even greater Medusan fury than usual by the icy blast outside, made him look truly manic.

'Ah, yes. I see what you mean. Perhaps we should look for a table,' said Esko, looking around more soberly. They began to move away from the door until Catrina spotted Mercedes waving.

'We could go back to my friend over there. She has space.' It was natural for Catrina to think that Mercedes was summoning her back, now that the Bruno threat had removed itself, but in fact the wave had been aimed at someone entirely different, as she discovered when they arrived at the back of the room and found the Scotsman divesting himself of all the winter coverings and settling down on the bench next to Mercedes. The point became even more obvious when they kissed.

The confusion of the last few minutes was making Catrina feel almost as out of control as Fidel – especially when the thought struck her that of the five people gathered at the table she was the only one any of them knew.

'Oh, sorry,' she began. It seemed a safe opening.

Mercedes looked up at her and grinned. 'I thought you were leaving?'

'Well, I—'

'I hope you are not going to be as rude to my friend as you were to poor Mariana's.'

'No, it's just that, you know, an ex is an ex and—'

Mercedes touched the arm of the man next to her. 'This is Rory. Now I'm hoping you don't know him at all.'

It was Rory that answered. 'Rory McBain. No, I'm sure we've never met.'

The introductions carried on as Catrina gestured to Esko and Fidel. Esko then took charge, guiding Fidel into the seat opposite Mercedes. 'Perhaps it would be best if I found us all some drinks. I've had enough coffee today. I'm moving on to beer. Anybody else?' That seemed to solve the immediate problem for everyone. 'In the mean time, you need to see what you can do for Fidel.' Esko headed for the bar.

Fidel was struggling with English, so Catrina switched to French as she explained to Mercedes. 'You remember Elise?'

'Of course.'

'She's had an accident, skiing in Italy. She's in hospital in Bolzano and Fidel needs to get there as soon as he can.'

'Oh no! Poor Elise! When can he go?'

'Don't know.' Catrina switched backed to English. 'Frankly I don't think he has a clue.'

Artistic Judgement

Nobody's mood is improved by having to walk uphill in sleet and against the wind. Bruno and Mariana were no exception. Bruno had announced huffily that there was no point in waiting for a tram on a Sunday and they might as well walk back to his place in St Gilles, even if it was 'effing freezing'. It was hard to tell from Mariana's sniffs whether she was still crying after their exit from the Café Franck or whether the weather was just getting to her nose. Bruno had suspicions that she was crying, mainly because he assumed that a Finn should be immune to vile temperatures. Either way, he reasoned, there was not much he could do about it till he had got her home.

They tramped up the hill towards Avenue Louise, heads down and faces swathed in scarves up to the eyes. It was a steeper climb than Bruno remembered. He was not exactly a fitness freak and, had he not been trying to look tough to Mariana, would have hung out in the other café in Place Flagey, Le Pitch-Pin, until he had spotted the 81 tram poking its nose into the far side of the square.

Two thirds of the way up the street he paused to catch his breath. 'Hang on a minute.'

Mariana stopped, peered at him and shrugged, moving into the lee of the nearest doorway. She said nothing and Bruno couldn't gauge her expression under the scarves. It was lucky. If he had, her look of derision would have been colder than the icy water gathering on their clothes. Once Mariana decided to do something she did not need pauses.

Next to Mariana a door opened and a woman stepped out, dressed in a fur coat that was clearly real, probably mink, buttoned all the way to the neck, collar turned up so that it reached the chin. On the woman's head perched a matching hat. She glanced at the sheltering Mariana and pulled the door to.

'Ye Gods, what is that?' exclaimed Bruno, pointing.

'What's what?' asked Mariana, assuming that he probably meant the woman's hat. So did the woman herself, who froze in the act of putting her keys away in her elegant black leather handbag and glared at Bruno.

'That!' repeated Bruno, gesturing at the window behind Mariana. 'Total crap. I mean, it's not art, it's a black splodge.'

Mariana followed the direction of Bruno's finger to the painting in the window of the gallery against which she was sheltering. There was indeed a splodge in the middle of a large white canvas, as though a spider had landed in a pool of ink, but radiating from it were intricate lines of primary colours that occasionally coagulated into tiny skulls or nude figures tossed out from the black centre like pumice from a volcano.

Beside Mariana the woman swore loudly and at length in Russian. The terms she was using described in exquisite detail how she would dissect Bruno's manhood if she ever got his trousers down. It was Mariana's turn to freeze.

'I understood that,' she said quietly, preparing herself to defend Bruno's honour.

'I'm very glad you did,' answered the woman.

'What did she say?' asked Bruno.

Mariana switched back to English. 'It was Russian. It doesn't matter. You don't need to know.'

'Yes he does,' said the woman, switching to English herself.

'No he doesn't,' replied Mariana firmly, stepping forward and taking Bruno's arm.

The woman matched her step. 'Perhaps not in detail,' she admitted, 'but he does need to hear that he is an artistic delinquent if he cannot recognise a brilliant evocation of the nihilism in the spirit of winter when he sees it. Why would I otherwise put it in the window of my gallery?'

'Because, just like all arty-farty people, you can't recognise a total fraud when you see one,' Bruno laid in, 'or you're just part of the fraud, making gullible fools pay good money for utter rubbish.'

The woman was about to blaze, but instead just grinned. 'You are a very rude young man. You are also English, I think, and therefore have the mind of the *petit bourgeois*, always thinking of the price of the potatoes in the window of your little shop. I, on the other hand, am Russian, and I have in my shop window the work of artists who have something interesting to say, whether it is pretty or not. Here in Brussels there are enough people who agree with me that I am still here after three years and soon to be opening another gallery in Paris.'

She turned to Mariana. 'I suggest, my dear, that you consider your friend's views and manner carefully. I am Nikita. I hope to see you inside one day. You will find it much warmer.' With that Nikita adjusted her gloves and walked with as much poise as the wind would allow down the hill.

There was not much Bruno could say, but he said it anyway. 'Silly Russian cow.'

It was fatal. Mariana looked at him again with the disdain which few other nationalities can summon: a look of such neutrality that the object human might just be another mile of tundra.

'You are wrong. She is Russian, and I do not love Russians. But the other two words, no.' Without waiting for any further observations from Bruno she followed Nikita back down the hill towards Flagey.

Two things occurred to Bruno simultaneously. The first was that he might have put his foot in it. The second that there was a tram climbing the hill towards him. He was cold. His ears were stinging and his toes were numb. There was a simple enough choice to be made: peace with women or peace in his armchair. He could at least guarantee that there was warmth in the room that held the armchair, which was more than could be said for the hearts of the women. Not much of a choice really. Bruno darted across the street and waved the tram to a halt.

Towards the bottom of the hill Mariana was once more not quite sure whether there were tears or just rivers of sleet running down her face. Across the square she could see the fur-clad figure of Nikita approaching the door of Café Franck. She wanted to follow her in, tell her she was completely right to put Bruno in his place; that her eyes had been opened and what had seemed like virile certainty two hours ago now had been shown up as mere boorishness. If she did that, though, she would have to make peace with Catrina too and admit that her judgement of her countryman was entirely justified, painful as it had been at the time. Worse still, she would have to make the admission in front of Esko. With her history of emotional failure where he was concerned, she was not sure she was quite ready for that. Neither, though, was she ready to go home and mope alone.

Mariana reached the end of the street and procrastinated. She turned into the snug local retreat that was Le Pitch-Pin.

Fidel Is Unsociable

By mid-afternoon Patrice was finishing his shift behind the bar and was ready to go home and do nothing very much for the rest of Sunday. The place was packed, though, as if everybody who usually used it was spending the last weekend of the New Year downtime to regroup before the serious business of work began again the following morning. At the back Esko, Mercedes, Rory and Catrina sat, trying to sort out Fidel's transport problems. In front of them Agnestina leant on a radiator, played with her hair and browsed her computer.

Patrice sighed with relief as the barman from the late shift appeared at his elbow. Once the final glass of beer had been bought, he had a chance to untie his apron and hang it on the hooks next to the back office. He retrieved his warm jacket and made his way over to Catrina.

'Shall we go?' he suggested, leaning over her and giving her shoulders a hug.

Catrina looked up and smiled. 'Soon,' she said, 'but we need to get Fidel to Elise first.'

'To Elise? She is in Italy.'

'Yes.'

'So why does Fidel need to get there so suddenly?'

'Oh hell, we should have told you, but you were out the back.'

'Told me what?'

'Elise has had a bad fall skiing. She's in hospital in Bolzano with broken… Well, we're not sure what she has broken, but it's bad enough for her to be having an operation today.'

'*Merde!*' Patrice pulled up a chair. 'What shall we do?'

'For now we are just trying to get Fidel out there. The nurse rang and asked him to come, but it's not the easiest place to get to in a hurry,' Catrina admitted.

'Is there an airport?'

'Yes, but it's not exactly the hub of Europe.'

Esko looked up from the screen of his phone. 'I'm trying to search. It would be easier with a laptop.'

'We could use the office, but if the manager needs it…' Patrice looked around him and spotted Agnestina. 'I wonder…' He stood up and went over, returning with her a few seconds later. 'This is Agnestina. She is happy to help,' he said.

The others looked at her appraisingly as she settled on to the bench seat next to Esko and cleared space on the table for her laptop. Mercedes realised she had seen her before – at least she had noticed her hair and been riven with jealousy. Catrina thought she had that French delicate beauty that no English woman could ever match and was instantly wary – glancing at Patrice for any evidence of dangerous familiarity. Esko thought of Amelie and hoped this new girl had no pretensions to being an actress. Only Fidel cared nothing, staring into his beer and waiting for someone to solve his crisis.

'I have explained the problem to her,' Patrice told them. Agnestina smiled her hallo and logged herself into a couple of travel websites. 'While she is looking, I'll get us some drinks.' Patrice, professional as he was, took in at a glance what everybody was having and headed back to the bar.

After a few moments clicking and gazing at the screen Agnestina looked up. 'Do you need to go tonight?' she asked Fidel. 'It is not easy. You will spend many hours waiting in an airport between flights, or in a station for the slow trains. It will be better if you go early tomorrow.'

Fidel looked at her without interest. He had not taken her existence in at all. 'If you say so.'

'What are his options?' asked Esko.

'He has to change in Frankfurt, whatever he does,' Agnestina said. He can either fly and then change again in Innsbruck…' She clicked between websites.

'Or?' Catrina prompted.

'Or he can go by train. It takes almost the same route, but if he catches the ICE fast trains there is not much difference in time, if you add in all the getting to and waiting in airports. And he will be nearer the hospital when he gets there.'

Esko and Patrice looked at Agnestina in new admiration. She was clearly competent as well as gorgeous. Catrina just nodded. Mercedes, though, was not watching. She was staring over their heads towards the door.

'Oh, there's Nikita. I must say a happy New Year.' Again it was Esko, Rory and Patrice, the least involved in Fidel's woes, who turned and followed the Catalan with their eyes as she rose and went to meet her employer. Many of those at other tables were watching too, drawn not by Nikita herself but by the politically incorrect extravagance of the fur coat and hat.

'She looks as though she is going to meet the Tsar,' muttered Esko drily.

'Then I'd better act the perfect servant,' grinned Patrice, and rose to take her order before she had to queue.

Nikita played the great lady to perfection. She waited for Patrice to find her a double espresso and a large cognac before letting Mercedes lead her and him back to the table. On cue Esko rose and rearranged the seating. Catrina was convinced he even bowed slightly.

'My dears,' uttered Nikita in collective greeting. She removed her coat and let Esko fold it carefully on to the banquette beside her. The hat stayed where it was, firmly set over the equally firm blonde hair. Not for the first time Esko wondered how old she was. Her manner, her dress, her exaggerated make-up all proclaimed her as a woman in her mid to late forties, but her face, beneath all the treatment, suggested she was younger – perhaps ten years younger. Usually a worked-on appearance was applied to convince onlookers that youth was still at hand; in Nikita's case it seemed to be the opposite – as though she had adopted an image of an age she wanted to be and was slowly growing her way towards it.

She inclined her head as Patrice placed the coffee and cognac in front of her. Mercedes hovered, not knowing quite where to sit now her old place had been usurped, until Patrice rescued her by joining two tables together and pulling across chairs for them both.

'And how are we all this New Year, the day before my Christmas?' Nikita asked. 'There are some here I don't know, I think.' She placed her fingers on Fidel's arm, expected him to dissolve beneath her charm. He did not even turn, instead concentrating his eyes on the back of Agnestina's computer as though it would transform into a magic carpet and glide him over the Alps.

Mercedes introduced her to Rory then explained the situation while Esko and Agnestina continued trying to work out the easiest journey for Fidel.

'How did Elise get there herself?' asked Catrina.

'I have no idea,' admitted Fidel. 'I think she went with her brother.'

'Do you have his number?'

Fidel shook his head.

'Agnestina will need your credit and identity card numbers to book the tickets,' Catrina went on. 'Do you have them?'

Fidel began to search for his wallet, trawling through his pockets, each a mystery. Catrina, who spent a disproportionate amount of her life hunting for lost treasure in her shaggy bag (an activity which had been the catalyst that had brought to a bitter end her relationship with Bruno), sympathised. By the time Fidel produced the cards and laid them apologetically by Agnestina's hand she was at the train booking page and Mercedes had finished the story for Nikita.

The Russian put her hand on Fidel's arm again. 'Will you be all right on this journey tomorrow?'

Fidel's expression was dull with fear and resignation. 'I must be. If Elise...'

'Do you speak German and Italian?'

'No. Only French and Flemish – perhaps a little English.'

Nikita turned to Mercedes. 'You speak everything, don't you darling?'

'Not quite everything.'

'Yes, I know – nothing Slav, but quite enough for Bolzano and Frankfurt. Darling, you must take him. I was going to keep the gallery closed this week anyway. Nobody buys pictures this early in January.'

'But how… I mean, I can't…' Mercedes glanced in panic at Rory. 'Not tomorrow.'

'You can – and I can go with you too,' Rory said, seizing his chance. 'There's nothing happening in my office I can't postpone for a few days or deal with online.'

'But it's so expensive!' protested Mercedes.

'Ridiculous, darling,' said Nikita. 'We'll do it on the gallery's card. I need to invent some expenses for it, in any case, if I am to make a satisfactory loss for the tax people.'

'I didn't hear that,' Esko said firmly. Expenses in Italy (his former colleague's – not his own) were a sore point in his political life.

'Of course, you didn't. And,' Nikita continued to Mercedes, 'I may join you at the weekend.' She smiled, warming to the new idea. 'We could all go!'

Bivouac

The weather was not getting any better. As afternoon became evening the sleet turned to heavy snow and, if it was not as immediately penetrating as the sleet, it was just as cold. The Brussels pavements were soon skating rinks. Bruno paused for breath and tried to find shelter at the tram stop on Avenue Louise. The tram he had taken a few minutes before had yet again stopped short of its usual destination and dumped him out instead of taking him all the way home – another conspiracy. He knew that he would be covered in snow by the time another one came. There was hope from another direction, though. To the south-east he could see the distant lights of a 94 trundling along the endlessly straight boulevard. He waited until the lights were only a junction away before he swapped platforms, which meant leaving the rudimentary shelter he had found against the blizzard. At least this way he could be warm for two stops and then two more on the metro before he reached home.

He stepped into the tram and sat down with relief, cherishing the heaters as the doors closed. The tram speakers trilled. '*Prochain arrêt, Stephanie.*' Then, immediately, the voice of the driver cut in. 'Final stop, Stephanie.' Bruno swore fiercely. Not only was that one stop short of the metro, it meant he had wasted a fare going just one stop twice in a few minutes. Then he realised he had not scanned his card yet. He would travel free the few hundred metres to Place Stephanie. It was minor revenge on the Brussels transport tribunes.

A few seconds later he was out in the snow again. He crossed the street from the tram tracks to the pavement and promptly slithered on to his bottom – betrayed by the shiny slope of the angled stones that formed a taxi way into the circular drive and the wedding-cake grandeur of the Conrad Hotel – the hotel where, a few months earlier, Amelie had holed up from reporters as news of her affair with Esko broke.

An elderly woman in acres of wool helped him to his feet. 'You must be more careful, monsieur,' she clucked, 'and wear the right shoes for this weather.' Bruno was mortified – firstly because he was being hauled upright by a woman twice, if not three times, his age; secondly because he could hardly admit that he only had two pairs of shoes and they were identical, both with smooth leather soles, as befitted his idea of an English gentleman. The fact that a true English gentleman would have been the first to reach for the second pair of socks and the Wellington boots, or at least stout brogues, when venturing out in January failed to occur to him.

'Thanks,' he mumbled, and wandered off in the opposite direction to the old woman. As he had fallen, so his coat had floated upwards, and the seat of his trousers was now both sopping and freezing. Bruno felt thoroughly sorry for himself – even worse when he realised that, in trying to stride away from his rescuer, he was actually walking back the way he had just travelled on the tram.

Bruno swore again.

In front of him the red carpet and overhanging canopy of the Hotel Bristol beckoned. Bruno glanced in the plate-glass window. Behind comfortable and empty sofas a man, business-like but dressed in Sunday casuals, gazed back at him from the bar. Bruno had a sudden and irresistible urge to join the world of credit card expenses. He turned into the hotel, ignored the inquisitive look from the plump uniformed receptionist – there was no room to check into or guest to meet – and turned to the bar.

The barman, tall, slender and vaguely middle-eastern, looked at the bedraggled figure, and correctly picked English as the right language. 'You are wet, Monsieur. Perhaps you would like to hang your coat up over there?' He indicated a line of hooks on the back wall. Bruno nodded and did so. When he returned, the comment was repeated. 'You are still wet, monsieur.'

'Yes, I am. I fell over in the snow just now.'

'That is unfortunate. You are staying here at the Hotel Bristol?'

'No.'

'That is even more unfortunate. You cannot easily slip, as you would say in English, into something more comfortable.'

'Or dry.'

'Precisely. Nevertheless there is a heater by the wall which may help, and in the mean time perhaps I could bring you some of my own recipe spiced *vin chaud* to ease your distress?'

This was exactly the way Bruno had always wanted barmen to talk to him. He could feel his anger evaporating almost as fast as the water that began to steam from his trousers while he leant against the tall radiator. 'Thank you. That would be great.'

The barman bowed and began the ceremony of preparing a glass saucer on the bar with spoon, sugar and two thin dark chocolates. From a covered punch bowl mounted over a candle he ladled a steaming glassful. 'Monsieur.' He bowed again and pushed the wine close enough to Bruno so that he could drink and steam by the radiator at the same time.

Bruno sipped, stirred in two lumps of sugar and sipped again. A little later, towards the bottom of the glass, he was aware both that his trousers were no longer wet – indeed, they were pleasantly warm – and that the *vin chaud* had a little more in it than hot plonk. Maybe there was brandy in there, or a dash of port. Whatever the secret, he found he was smiling.

'Monsieur is feeling better, I think,' said the barman as he deftly cleared the glass, though careful to leave the wrapped slivers of chocolate on the counter. 'Maybe another will restore you to full health?'

'Maybe,' admitted Bruno. 'I'll only know when I've tried it.'

'Then we must continue to experiment.'

Bruno settled himself on to a bar stool, unwrapped and nibbled a chocolate, and looked out to the street. Night had fallen in the time he had drunk his wine, and by the hotel lights he could see that the snow was settling nicely. He turned back to the bar as his fresh glass was placed beside him with a flourish – though with peanuts rather than chocolates as the extra titbit. Three stools down the businessman in casuals – grey winter slacks and a pullover of ochre lambswool – gestured to the barman that he needed a refill too. He turned to the now-grinning Bruno.

'You living out here?' he asked in an accent that was one of the milder American variety.

Bruno nodded.

'Working?'

'Yes, over at the European Parliament,' Bruno said.

'Member?'

'Sadly not – at least, not yet. I hope to be a candidate next time. Just an assistant at the moment.'

The American looked at him thoughtfully as three fingers of bourbon over ice was put between his hands. 'Maybe we can do business.'

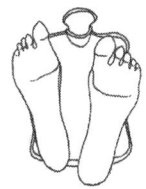

And So to Bed

'Tyron Wangstrutt.'

'I beg your pardon?'

'My name.'

'Really! How?'

'What do you mean, how?'

'I mean, how does a name like that happen?'

'Well, hell, I guess my Mom didn't know there's an *e* on the end of Tyrone and Wangstrutt's a name you'll find all over that part of Missouri. So what's yours?'

'Bruno Inchcombe.'

'See?'

'See what?'

'Sounds pretty strange to me.'

The businessman and Bruno stared into their drinks and mulled over the strangeness of the world while the snow fell heavily, quickly coating the cars parked outside the Hotel Bristol in a thick and frozen duvet. Both men were discovering that their continents were as far apart as they were respectively from Central Asia, whatever the illusion of a partly shared language. Bruno regarded American names as simply funny; Tyron found the Englishman's absurdly quaint (itself a word that had changed its meaning utterly over the centuries).

'But heck, who cares!' Tyron announced. 'Let's have another drink.'

'Why not?'

The barman obeyed the summons with alacrity. These were his only customers and, on a miserable Sunday evening in January, were likely to be until much later when the last Eurostar train from London had disgorged its cargo of those not wanting to get up fiendishly early to beat the time difference for Monday morning meetings.

'Why not' was also the phrase going through the minds of two other Parliamentary assistants that lonely evening before the work of the year began. Down the hill in Place Flagey, Mariana was discovering her Finnish soul in demi-carafes of white Burgundy, occasionally sharing a nondescript comment on the awfulness of weather, of men, of Belgium and the world with her host behind the bar, a lady called Yseult who looked as though she could have been anywhere between forty and fifty but was in fact only thirty-seven, like Nikita. Life had been unsatisfactory. Whereas Nikita looked older by design, in Yseult's case it was through troubles.

She and Mariana both had taken a look at the blizzard and concluded that smoking in Le Pitch-Pin in defiance of new laws was unlikely to stir anyone's wrath, especially since the four elderly men playing cards in the far corner had been doing so all afternoon.

A few hundred metres up the hill on the other side of the square, Saskia van Katwijk (what would Tyron and she make of each other's names?) had none of the solace of a stranger's companionship as she edged towards the bottom of her second bottle of Orvieto. The entertainment of drawing caricatures of the main aggravations in her life had palled after an hour or two, and she had found herself watching women's tennis from Australia, wondering in a vague and tipsy way whether she cared who won and whether it mattered if she could watch and undress at the same time, while already in bed with the electric blanket set to medium roast. After a moment of brow-furrowing she decided she didn't care and it didn't matter. Somewhere around the start of a third set between girls with big thighs she'd never heard of, who screeched in pain every time they swung a racket, Saskia managed to unbutton and take off her jeans before warmth and sporting tedium arranged for her to sleep.

By the time Fidel had been escorted back to his flat he was fully in the Russian mothering care of Nikita, whether he liked it or not. She had despatched Mercedes to the station to pick up their train tickets so that they did not have to queue in the morning. It was going to be an early enough start, with the fast train to Frankfurt leaving shortly after six. Mercedes would accompany Fidel, as would Rory, who had initially thought he couldn't get away from work despite his confident promise to Mercedes, but after two phone calls found that nobody much cared.

Fidel's flat was in its usual state of chaos – in fact, worse than usual, because he had been without the steadying hand of Elise for so many days. Nikita came in, looked around, sniffed, walked through to the kitchen and grinned. She had brothers in St Petersburg just like this. It always encouraged her to find that her assumptions about the male character were accurate. She made Fidel sit down in his armchair and gave him the sole task of deciding which papers and books were going to be essential for his journey. She knew that in his current state of bewildered anxiety that was going to be quite enough.

She made tea, washed up the accumulated dishes, then (without asking permission from the man she had met less than five hours before) went through to the bedroom and began to sort out his clothes. Those on the floor she shoved straight into a plastic rubbish sack, ready to be taken to her house and laundered. She found a case with zips that seemed to function and packed enough clothes for ten days, including extra socks for the mountains and changes of jumpers and jackets that Fidel might not choose to wear, but which she had a notion Elise would have guided him towards.

Mercedes arrived back by half-past seven, having picked up the tickets and stopped off at her own flat to pack and print out the booking slips for the hotel reservation. She and Nikita agreed that it would be sensible for Mercedes to sleep in Elise's flat that night to make getting to the station halfway through it easier, especially in the snow. Rory had been deputed to meet Fidel and Mercedes with a taxi at five the next morning.

Fidel, still in a daze, surrendered his spare key to Elise's rooms one floor below, and Mercedes entered them with rather more reverence than Nikita had Fidel's. Thereafter, though, she performed much the same service, for Elise was not a lot tidier than her lover. Packing was easier: just the few extra underclothes, T-shirts and books in French that would be needed for the days in hospital.

By nine that night the snow was so enveloping that even Patrice decided he had better go back to his own place for different clothes if he was to make it into work early. Catrina was left to re-establish the arrangements for bed that had seen her through so many Derbyshire winters: thick flannel pyjamas, thick, sweet dark cocoa, those extra socks she had so stupidly left off the night before, and two hot water bottles.

In Bolzano Elise slept the sleep of the deeply sedated. For the lovers, enemies and acquaintances who had come together in Flagey it was a strange night, for they all slept alone.

III

Monday

A Jolt to Routine

First thing on the first Monday back at work after the Christmas and New Year hiatus could be counted on to be quiet, Catrina reckoned, as she touched her pass against the security gates of the European Parliament five minutes before nine o'clock. She would have been doing it ten minutes earlier if the Parliament's administration had not decided to change the entrance location, pass-reading mechanisms and entire security staff over the holidays. The result was one queue that stretched out into the snow and another that huddled under the arch between the two halves of the building. There the snow had only drifted to an icy crust, but the arch formed a wind tunnel, so the choice was between cold feet or cold faces.

The heating inside did not seem to have failed, at least, and once inside Catrina began to unwind the scarf, drop down her coat hood and stow gloves and ear muffs on the way to the lift. Halfway to the tenth floor she heard her mobile beep. She pulled it from the recesses of her hairy Afghan bag and glanced at the screen.

'Hell!' she announced, eliciting a raised eyebrow and the twitch of a smile from her lift companions. The text was straightforward:

Back to the fray see you in an hour Gw.

In other words, her employer, Gwyneth Price MEP (Plaid Cymru/Green group) would not be arriving in the middle of the afternoon as was the normal Monday pattern, but had come back early and was in the city already. What sort of journey from Machynlleth on a Sunday that would have entailed, Catrina dreaded to think. Or maybe Gwyneth had done the same as Esko and spent the weekend in Brussels, escaping the suffocation of family. Catrina wondered idly whether Gwyneth too had a secret lover on the continent. It seemed unlikely. Gwyneth was a woman for whom the word homely could have been invented – full of figure (though not more than plump), sensible in clothes, shoes and hair. Although her voice – ringing, brisk and with a hint of bite in the enunciation – gave the lie to the idea that she was an average housewife, Catrina could not quite bring herself to imagine her as an object of illicit passion – but of course one never knew.

Either way, she would be in the office at ten.

Catrina slumped into her office chair, flicked on the computer and looked disconsolately between the forest of emails and the distressing pile of papers she had placed neatly on the left of the desk in mid-December, subconsciously convinced that mid-January would never come, but that if it did the pile would have evaporated into the political clouds. As it was, January had arrived, the papers had survived and nearly three hundred emails suggested urgency. Luckily more than half were in Welsh and could be simply forwarded on to the nice lady in the Cambrian mountains who dealt with such things.

Procrastination was called for. Catrina could procrastinate constructively, though. She would grab a large coffee and collect the accumulated letters from the post room as well.

By the time Gwyneth sailed into the room on the dot of ten Catrina had filled a recycling bag with envelopes, sorted out the invitations from the circulars and general-information flyers and arranged the pertinent ones on her boss's desk. She had also printed out half-dozen emails that Gwyneth needed to see before Catrina answered. The rest she had forwarded to the various political and Welsh assistants. The secret of working happily in an MEP's office was to shield her or him from eighty per cent of the incoming words – to find ten per cent worth glancing at and ten per cent that really needed to be talked about, and know which was which. The rest could be deleted.

Gwyneth came round the desk and nodded approvingly. 'Been here long?' she asked with a smile.

'Only since I got your text.' Catrina's suspicion that her patron had spent the night in Brussels was confirmed by the lack of the familiar green suitcase that Gwyneth usually dragged behind her when travelling.

'You've been busy. Thanks. How was Christmas?'

'Great – I mean, you know…'

'Only too well. It's over, thank heavens. Do anything fun for New Year?'

Catrina grinned. 'Came back – to Patrice.'

'Lucky you. I was stuck doing good works till Wednesday, then got snowed in for three days. I had a hell of a journey yesterday to get back here.'

'I thought you might.'

'Worth it, though.' Gwyneth did not elaborate, to Catrina's chagrin. 'Let's get through this lot, then. Sorry to start on real work so soon, but if we can get everything out of the way there's a chance I can be ahead of the game. Then I want to have lunch with you. I've got stuff to tell.'

A few minutes later, while both women – fortified with more coffee – contemplated their computers and papers in silence, the text tone on Catrina's mobile buzzed again. The message was from Mercedes:

Just left Frankfurt. Fidel a mess but we made it. Text you when we get to IT.

Catrina wrote back:

Thanks. Good luck. ☺

She would have to tell Gwyneth the story later, since, even after the holidays, it looked as though she had to take off for a long weekend.

At lunch, in the members' dining room for once, rather than the canteen, Gwyneth ordered them both glasses of white wine – very out of character, but Catrina was not going to object. 'Are we celebrating?'

'I suppose we are. It's the start of my second year here…'

Catrina suspected that was not the real excuse. 'And?'

'And I have some help coming into the office from Wednesday: a boy who can look after my political side – the green and nationalist bits, not the EU parts that you do so well.'

'Fine. What's his name?'

'Dylan. Dylan Morris. Been six months out of uni, so he should be prepared to do some work.'

'OK.'

'And I'm getting married.'

It was a few seconds before Catrina realised she was staring at Gwyneth with her mouth open and her glass halfway to her lips. 'Sorry?'

'It's not that astounding, is it? I mean, I'm not that much of a gargoyle, am I?'

'No, no, of course not. It's just—'

'Anyway, you can judge whether he's mad or I'm mad soon enough. He'll be here in a minute.'

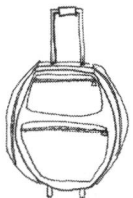

Early Trains

As far as he was thankful for anything as he relaxed into his seat on the ICE high-speed train for Innsbruck at Frankfurt, Fidel was thankful that Mercedes was with him. He was still not quite sure who Mercedes was, or why she and this

Scotsman called Rory were coming all the way to Bolzano with him. That they had taken the trouble to pick him up from his flat at five in the morning, had arrived with tickets paid and printed and had treated him as if he was an extremely aged gentleman in social care.

Maybe that was what he was.

The news that his twenty-something girlfriend Elise was lying in hospital in Italy had certainly shocked him into a state of helplessness which now filled him with acute embarrassment. Yet it was true that, at only a modest fifty plus a few, the modern demands for instant action had left him floundering. It had taken a Finn, a Russian, an Englishwoman, a Belgian barman and student, a Spaniard and a Scotsman to organise his dash to Elise's bedside. Had he had to recover and figure it out for himself, Fidel acknowledged with shame, it would have taken at least a day longer.

With barely a shudder the sleek white train began to pull away from the platform. Fidel realised the Scotsman was looking at him.

'Feeling better now?' asked Rory, sensibly using French.

'A little,' Fidel admitted. They had not spoken much on the previous, very similar, train from Brussels to Frankfurt. Apart from the early start and the freezing weather, there seemed nothing worth talking about at that hour of a Monday morning. They had berthed themselves and drifted back to sleep, Fidel against the carriage wall, Mercedes and Rory against each other. Now, nearing a tolerable time on this second train, conversation felt possible and his self-confidence was returning.

'That's good. I'll go and see if I can find coffee. I'm sure we could all do with it,' said Rory. He smiled and made his way back along the carriage. They had managed to reserve seats facing each other with a table in between for this second leg of the journey.

Fidel studied Mercedes for a moment. 'Forgive me,' he began. 'You are both being very kind, but why exactly are you coming with me to see Elise?'

It was, Mercedes realised, a good question. 'My boss, Nikita, who owns the gallery, thought I could help since the gallery is closed this week.'

Fidel nodded. 'She was right. This would have been hard for me. And the Scottish gentleman?'

'Oh, Rory just thought it would be fun – and Nikita is paying, so it is a free trip to the Dolomites.'

'I see,' said Fidel, not seeing at all. He thought of an explanation. 'Do you know Elise well?'

'Not especially – only from the café.'

'But you still came. I am amazed – there is no other word for it.'

In truth Mercedes was a little amazed too. A day before she had been expecting to be spending this morning opening up the gallery and settling back into Brussels work life, not starting on a week-long trip to an Italian ski resort with Rory, and in the company of this dishevelled Belgian professor.

'And your friend, Rory… have you known him long?'

'Not long,' admitted Mercedes. 'In fact, only since New Year.'

'So this is all, what can I say, very sudden?'

'I suppose it is,' Mercedes agreed doubtfully, thinking that, for her, the last week or so felt like an age and that her life now divided into two parts: Rory and Pre-Rory.

'So you work in the gallery with Nikita. And Mr… forgive me, I do not even know his other name.'

'McBain…'

'Mr McBain – is he there too?'

'No, no!' Mercedes grinned at the thought of Rory and Nikita trying to share an office. 'He's a journalist. He writes for *Europe Now*.'

'Ah…' Fidel was never quite sure how he felt about journalists. On the one hand that was how he too earned much of his living, although he would make the distinction that he was an essayist and critic, not a reporter; on the other he had always been terrified of being on the wrong end of a story.

Rory returned carrying a bag of coffee cups and ham rolls. 'I was just explaining that you are a journalist,' said Mercedes as he sat down and started to distribute the refreshments.

'Aye, that's right, though nobody seems to think there'll be much to write about in Brussels this week, so the editor has been happy enough to pack me off with you. He's told me to look out for a nice background piece on how the other half lives for winter sports – see if I can spot any politicians having an après-ski with someone surprising.'

'I thought your newspaper was more serious than that,' Fidel muttered.

'It is, most of the time. But it's January, first issue after New Year, and nobody wants to be reminded of just how much work they have ahead of them yet. So a little bit of atmosphere writing won't hurt. Anyway, if there had been a crisis brewing I wouldn't be with you now.'

It was a truth Fidel was prepared to acknowledge. 'I am pleased you are. Thank you. Today may be very difficult.'

That thought was enough to make them all lapse into silence. On Fidel's side of the table it was an uneasy journey as he veered between fears for Elise and worries about his assumed resignation from his university, according to Sunday's Belgian papers. There had been no time to clarify the real position. He could, of course, just call the department on his mobile as he sped through the German, and then the Austrian, countryside, but he didn't, justifying his inaction on the reasonable grounds that there was nothing useful he could say until he found out how things were in Bolzano. And this Rory man might report what he overheard. It was a delusional point, but just at that moment delusions were what Fidel needed most.

Harsh Morning

There was one characteristic shared by Saskia, Mariana and Bruno as they queued at different counters for coffee in Parliament that January Monday, and it was one they would rather not have shared – though there was a good chance Mariana would have wished it on Bruno had she known: a hangover.

Mariana's was the fault of the uncountable small glasses of unidentifiable white Burgundy she had drunk at Le Pitch-Pin in the process of trying to wipe Bruno out of her memory. Not all of it had been bought by her. In fact, very little of it. She had been helped on the way to morning ruin by Yseult, the diminutive Breton barmaid, and given a hefty push when she was joined by the oppositely proportioned Louise Camille who, like Mariana, had adopted the little bar by the tram stop when she was fed up with Café Franck across the square of Flagey. Had she known it (but the matter had never come up, though it could have done when Mariana revealed that she worked for an MEP), Louise was something else she shared with Saskia, though in nothing like the same way.

The three women (Louise, Mariana and Yseult) had sat and smoked and talked and drank until all the men had given up and drifted home in the Sunday night snow. They would probably have carried on long after, but some time towards midnight Louise had announced that she was being sensible. She had offered hospitality at her flat just round the corner of the lake, but Yseult and Mariana had thought about it, looked at the snow and declined. They lived, they found, a fair distance from each other, but Yseult's taxi, a perk from the boss on such a night as this, would take her past Mariana's door. That single moment of sense, however, came too late to prevent the hangover.

Saskia's pain was entirely self-inflicted. She had snacked, played online, flicked through YouTube, watched the snow a little and somewhere around the end of a bottle (indeed the second) of Orvieto, had fallen asleep with the TV on, playing tennis. At three in the morning she had woken and switched off the screen. The night fairies had her by the throat, though. They brought in all her fears to torment her – the fears that never dared show in daylight. She made herself a tumbler of hot whisky, carried the laptop with her back to bed and left the lights on. She slept again as the morning trams started down Rue Malibran and tentative traffic began to slither on the treacherous frozen streets.

Bruno woke at home in St Gilles, but that was more by luck than judgement. After the barman at the Hotel Bristol had suggested mulling another cauldron of fortified wine, the American at the far end of the counter had moved up a few feet, ordered hamburgers from the night kitchen for them both, and announced that all future fare would be put down as parliamentary entertainment on his expense account. To mulled wine had been added bourbon and brandies, and by half-past ten in the evening Bruno was barely able to stay upright on his bar stool.

His new best friend, the American Tyron Wangstrutt, had been solicitous, even going as far as to offer Bruno a room for the night in the Hotel Bristol, all courtesy of his company, the name of which Bruno was sure Wangstrutt had mentioned somewhere along the line, but which had utterly escaped him when he tried to free the memory cell. Deep in Bruno's befuddled brain caution had overcome the temptation of a serviced bed and he had found himself being guided to a taxi by the barman before his legs gave out completely.

To be fair to Wangstrutt, Bruno thought, simultaneously noting that the coffees in Parliament were too small, the Yank had given him twenty euros for the taxi.

The coffee was the final stage of the hangover victory plan. Earlier stages had involved a bacon baguette, two maximum-strength ibuprofen tablets and two cans of coke. Bruno was not sure he was winning.

Neither was Mariana. She knew she could face neither Esko's concern nor the smug glow of her colleagues' New Year cheerfulness. She dumped her coat on the office chair, switched on her computer then, grabbing her bag in the unspoken declaration of a woman suffering her period, disappeared to the ladies' toilet for an hour. She would have to come up with a good medical excuse the following week, when her period really was due. She swore at herself in the relative dark.

Saskia was made of sterner stock – or at least, good Brabant farmer stock, and refused to be inconvenienced by anything as trivial as a sore head and mild nausea. She merely glared at her employer, daring him to comment as she shut the office door after the most perfunctory of New Year greetings. Had she known it, his hangover was even worse than hers and the last thing he had wanted was a dose of Ms van Katwijk's merciless efficiency. Saskia quickly realised, though, that she was likely to be ill over her keyboard if she looked at it unshielded. Thus it was that she was the only person in Parliament on that grey and listless winter morning wearing dark glasses at her desk.

Soon after midday Bruno's mobile trilled, and he opened his eyes with reluctance and hauled himself upright from the recovery position he had collapsed into – leaning back as far as he could in the neck-high chair he had borrowed from his Member's half of the office.

The number was not one he recognised. 'Yes?' he answered without enthusiasm.

'Bruno. It's Tyron.'

'Ah.'

'I'm downstairs at this goddam security post. I've got a noon appointment with your man, remember?'

The momentary panic eased from Bruno's body. 'Not my man, thank heavens.'

'Really? No kidding!'

''Fraid not.'

'But your man is Belstead, Vice-President, Defence Commission?'

'No, Sanderson – External Relations.' Bruno grinned as far as the pain would let him. Belstead had been Catrina's old boss before jumping ship to Ms Price. Bruno would have enjoyed inflicting Tyron on her this morning.

'Hell. Must have got the numbers written down wrong. But I want to see him too.'

'Not here till late this afternoon. Sorry. Do you want me to find you Belstead's extension?'

'Great.'

Bruno managed to focus long enough to find the right line in the directory and put Wangstrutt on the right track.

'Any chance of seeing your guy this evening?'

'I doubt it. I've got your number. I'll text you when I've spoken to him. Will tomorrow do?'

'Yeah, I could make that.'

Bruno's brow furrowed. 'What did you say your organisation was?'

'You can tell him Ziggie Industries. He'll get it.'

'Right.' Bruno swiped off his phone and lay back once more, feeling the last vestige of energy draining through his jaw. He gave up the pretence of working, locked both office doors and curled himself on the hard grey sofa. For two hours he slept.

In Conclave

At three o'clock in the afternoon of Monday the 8th of January, committee room G-13 of the European Parliament's Brussels building was hardly bustling. A room designed to hold upwards of sixty MEPs and about the same number again of auxiliaries and assorted officials, together with a semi-circle of interpreters behind the first floor screens, had only twenty-five people shambling in, looking a little shell-shocked to be back from holiday.

All were members of SLEE – the centre-left political group that collectively thought of themselves as Social and Liberal, and as defenders of the often competing concepts of Enterprise and Ecology. There were indeed gaps in their political philosophy that their opponents described as making it incoherent, yet it was attractive too – and if there were times when finding a straight line between them required an exercise in dialectic that would have had the French intellectuals of Jean-Paul Sartre's generation rubbing their pens with glee, they were not a group that many in the firmament of European politics (except the nationalists of the far right) actively disliked. This may also have been because at full strength there were only thirty of them.

Esko Nystrom looked down from his President's chair with gloom. He would have preferred to sit among his colleagues, but the layout of the room made it impossible; at floor level he would neither see nor hear what was going on, which would not be a good start. He would have preferred too not to have been the new leader at all, but he was, and this first meeting of the parliamentary term would be, he knew, crucial to the future of his reign.

It was a meeting to which only the members themselves were invited – at least, for the first hour and a half. There were to be no staff – no assistants or researchers – allowed in;

not even the group's secretariat provided by the parliamentary authorities. The Secretary only would be admitted at half-past four to minute the conclusions and outline the official work for the weeks ahead. In the mean time that meant the members could talk unhindered by the niceties of public positions or party interest. It also meant, Esko reflected with foreboding, that they could behave as obstructively to him as they liked.

He was the new boy. They would want to test him and jostle for position in the incoming regime. Esko's predecessor, the flamboyant Roberto Vincenzi, loved such meetings and the cut and thrust (sometimes almost literal) of party strife. Esko loathed them. He couldn't be bothered with intrigue, but intrigue was now his job.

Roberto had already told Esko that he would not be joining the meeting – indeed, he would not be in Brussels for two days yet, coming north from Rome just long enough to clock in to show he was still active. Being in the building now and again was important for the ex-leader if he wanted to be able to claim the temporary immunity from prosecution necessary while he fought the accusations of misappropriation that zealous prosecutors were throwing at him. In truth he was a gifted politician and an eloquent champion of liberty and fairness. He had never been, however, one of the world's natural accountants – never a problem in Italy until the current mood of democratic puritanism had taken over. The accusation that over ten years he had overlooked the true nature of €680,000 in his expenses was surely malicious. Roberto pointed out that being a successful politician in Italy was, always had been and always would be, a very expensive business. The purpose of expenses was to deal with things (and people) that were expensive. No?

At Esko's side was the woman who had pushed him into the group leadership, Brigitte Etzenberger; short-cropped blonde hair, black leather trousers and so tanned that she had clearly spent Christmas either so high up a mountain that the ozone was minimal or on a Caribbean beach. Esko was in no hurry to ask her which. He knew she would tell him at length anyway. His purpose in making her Deputy Leader was neither gratitude nor a genuflection to gender balance. If Brigitte was by his side she was likely to sit quietly, pass him notes and talk to him before and after meetings. If she was just one of the crowd she would inevitably take the floor and only relinquish it by force.

Esko gave the members five minutes to settle themselves then opened the meeting.

'Apparently you've elected me,' he said, smiling down. There were a few polite murmurs of approval. 'So I'll begin. As you know, it is the Leader's right in our group to choose a deputy – in fact, two deputies. As you can see, I've chosen Brigitte.' There were, it must be admitted, slightly less enthusiastic murmurs.

'Let me start by wishing everyone happy New Year – and then spoiling it by telling you that it might be a tough one for us. I'm sure that we all miss Roberto, but' – Esko was not going to wait for any dissent – 'there is no doubt that his predicament is going to be thrown at us by the press and every other group in this Parliament as often as they can. So I suggest that we make as few pronouncements as possible about political morality. Agreed?'

There was an embarrassed nodding. Several members just looked at their pencils.

'I hope you will have noticed,' Esko continued, 'that while I have nominated one deputy, I have not suggested a second. I think you should all be free to choose him or her without my influence. You might think of this as oddly democratic' – laughter – 'and you might think that it is because none of you are good enough' – no laughter – 'or perhaps just a sign of weakness on my part. I hope it is neither. There are plenty of able candidates. Nonetheless, I think we should take a few days to think about it and hold an election on Thursday at lunchtime.'

Esko paused for signs of dissent. Instead he saw members perk up, starting to look around for opportunities and allies.

'One thing...' he went on quietly, 'I suggest you think of appointing somebody from the south. We will need to explain ourselves around the Mediterranean a lot in the next few months, and I don't want this to look, as the Americans would say, like a stitch-up by the north. Now, to the business of the week.'

The general opinion at the end of the afternoon was that Esko had handled everything with just the right mixture of authority and consultation. The only person who felt depressed was Jens Sauer, the Luxembourger, who had assumed he would be everybody's favourite deputy, just as he had hoped he would be the obvious compromise leader. Since nobody could really claim that Luxembourg was in the south, he saw his hopes draining away. He would have to do something about it.

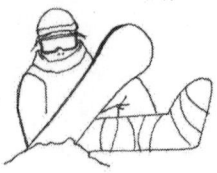

Hospital Visiting

Elise woke in the early afternoon and soon drifted back into sleep. The process, waking then sleeping, seemed to flow on timelessly. When she woke she would look about her, wonder where this white room with curtains was, wonder why people were talking softly in languages she couldn't catch, wonder why none of her limbs wanted to move. The answers were too far away, too complicated, and sleep claimed her again.

Eventually the periods of wakefulness began to lengthen, though she had no way of knowing whether those of sleep were shortening in parallel. And with each wakening she became aware that something hurt. No, that was not right – everything hurt, but somehow that didn't seem to matter very much. The pain was just there, in the same way that the bed was there, and the ceiling and the strange voices. There was a heaviness about her body that she couldn't understand. She had been a slight, indeed tiny, young woman, and now she thought this must be how it felt to be an old and very fat man. Everything hurt, nothing moved. Nothing could be done about it.

She was so thirsty, but nothing could be done to change that either. She saw there were pipes ending in her hand, but they carried no water and the thirst grew. Surely it was intolerable, like the pain. Maybe it would go if she slept again. Even as she thought it she plunged back into dreamless unconsciousness.

Once, when she came back, there was a woman holding her hand, checking the pipes. Elise whispered '*J'ai soif,*' but the woman just smiled and went away.

Each interlude between sleep was little different. Perhaps this was how life would be now: a parade of interludes in which nothing happened but pain, thirst and figures wandering among gentle lights.

She could think of nothing else. Maybe there was nothing else to think about.

Then a moment came when there was another hand holding hers, not checking pipes this time but just holding. She turned her head to look. That in itself was new. Before she had only stared at the ceiling, aware that people moved in the periphery of her vision. There was a man sitting beside her, looking very solemn. When he saw she was awake he half stood, leant forward and kissed her on the forehead.

'Elise,' he said.

'*J'ai soif,*' she said. Perhaps this man would succeed where the woman had failed. Elise slept again.

He was still there when she resurfaced, and this time he smiled, helped her raise her head and pressed a glass of water to her lips. After all the desperate thirst, though, she could only take a few sips – but that was enough; the thirst retreated. Only the pain remained. She wondered who this man was.

'Elise,' he said once more, though in reality there had been over half an hour between the words, 'I am here. It is me, Fidel. I love you so much.'

Slowly a cloud or two was lifting in her mind. She was pleased to see Fidel, she knew that, but she was not sure why.

It was nice that he loved her. She smiled and it didn't hurt. That was nice too.

'Where am I?'

Fidel stroked her cheek. 'You are in hospital – in Italy. You had a bad fall: very bad.'

'Oh.' Elise thought for a moment. 'But I don't live in Italy.'

'No – you are from Brussels.'

Elise nodded. That did hurt. She decided not to do it again. Then she said, 'And you are Fidel, and you love me, and you came here to tell me that after my fall.' Sleep came back, but somehow in her sleep there was a change, as though an important thing had returned in her mind.

A few minutes later a nurse appeared at the bedside. She nodded to Fidel, checked the drips and Elise's pulse, listened to her breathing through a stethoscope, then marked all the results on the chart hanging from the end of the bed.

'Signor…' she began, and followed with a gentle flow of Italian which left Fidel completely baffled. He sat still and smiled. The nurse repeated herself.

Fidel shrugged. '*Non parlo Italiano,*' he managed.

'*Ah, sì. Francese. Aspetta un'attimo.*' The nurse retreated, returning a couple of minutes later with a colleague who explained in heavily accented French that they would keep Elise sedated overnight, and perhaps it would be better if Fidel left now and came back in the morning, but not until after eleven. Yes, she knew he was worried, but the signs were good and he must expect the signorina not to be herself for a few days yet – the anaesthetic, the morphine and her concussion – he would understand. Fidel agreed sagely and, after a final kiss to Elise's sleeping head, allowed himself to be led away.

Outside the hospital the snow was falling steadily from clouds so low the mountains might never have existed. Fidel trudged back in the direction of the hotel Mercedes had checked them all into before dropping him off on his mission to Elise two hours earlier. At least he assumed it was the direction of his hotel. The street he wanted was by the river, he knew, and therefore downhill. What Fidel did not know was that Bolzano has two rivers that join to form the Adige, and he was working his way through the snow towards the wrong one.

After ten minutes he could barely feel his toes as the snow crept over and into his inappropriate shoes, and his ears and fingers felt certain to drop off. His Brussels winter coat was little defence against the mountain winter. A taxi was approaching and he hailed it but, once inside, found his linguistic fears defeated his attempt to explain where he wanted to go. Mercedes had foreseen that, however, and in his pocket Fidel felt the hotel card she had forced on him. The taxi driver glanced at it, muttered '*Pronto, signor*' and drove off. Fidel sank back gratefully, delighting in the car's heat as his glasses misted up.

They were still misted when they reached the hotel, and Fidel had to take them off to find the ten-Euro note for the fare. Once the change was given and the tip accepted, though, he put them back on to step out of the taxi on to the icy pavement.

The cry of warning from the driver came too late.

Fidel slithered and missed the taxi door as he tried to avoid the inevitable fall. The driver climbed out and came round to help his passenger up, invoking the saints and expressing all hope against hurt. A swift look at Fidel's ankle was enough.

Gingerly he bundled the stunned and grimacing Belgian back into the taxi, walked into the hotel to tell the receptionist of the accident and returned Fidel up the hill to the hospital from where he had just come. Which is where an anxious Mercedes and Rory found him an hour later as he emerged from X-ray.

Alliances Surprise

The man who appeared at Gwyneth Price's table in the members' restaurant as she and Catrina were helping themselves to more white wine that Monday lunchtime was not at all the sort of man Catrina was expecting. When her Plaid Cymru boss had announced she was getting married her natural assumption had been that it was to one or other of the Welshmen in Brussels – perhaps someone in the Commission or one of the myriad think-tanks. He would be comfy, like Gwyneth, possibly a little sturdy, with a twinkle, of course (Catrina couldn't imagine Gwyneth putting up for long with any man without a twinkle), but he would be of the same stuff.

Instead – and Catrina found it hard not to look amazed – Gwyneth was kissed by an elegant man in his early forties, very slim and immaculate in a dark woollen suit, white shirt and silk tie in green check, his luxuriant black hair swept back from his forehead in careful disorder. The twinkle was the only part left of her expectations.

Gwyneth preened. 'Catrina, this is Leontios. You won't want to try his second name.'

The man grinned and commented in accent-less English, 'The Welsh accusing the Greeks of being unpronounceable – now that is rich.' He pulled up a chair and poured himself a glass of what was left of the bottle of white wine. 'But I'm from Corfu, so my name is less complicated to the northern ear than some.'

'Um, ah…' Catrina mumbled. She didn't know quite where to begin – thinking, rightly, that to just say 'nice' would be utterly inadequate. Suddenly she felt very young. There was something dashing, Mediterranean and sophisticated about Leontios that made her feel she had stepped into a Fellini film. 'So you are going to marry Gwyneth?' The problem was trying to sound neither astonished nor incredulous. Catrina hoped it came out as just pleased.

'That is the plan. Of course, the lady always reserves the right to decide differently.'

'Oh, stop it!' exclaimed Gwyneth, almost purring. 'Catrina is feeling very English and a little out of her depth, aren't you dear?'

'No, no…' she lied.

'Leontios is one of our Greek friends on the Green left who is annoyed with what the bankers and the Germans are doing to his country.'

'I'm not surprised.'

'Neither, unfortunately, am I,' said Leontios, 'but I am pleased to say that my alliance with Gwyneth seems to run even deeper than politics.'

'Nice to know there is something deeper than politics. I sometimes wonder in this place,' said Catrina, the wine starting to bring out her acerbic side.

'But yes,' exclaimed Leontios – Catrina was starting to realise that he was a man who always exclaimed – 'otherwise we would never be at peace.'

'Are we at peace?' Gwyneth wondered.

'Probably not,' Leontios admitted, 'but at least we are not actively at war. You only have to look an hour's flight further east from Athens to see the difference. This is not the moment for such a discussion, though. Catrina, Gwyneth wanted you to meet me. I think she was nervous you would disapprove.' He smiled.

To Catrina's surprise her boss blushed. 'Not really. Do you?' she asked.

Catrina could have answered immediately and put her elders at their ease. Instead she took a long sip of her wine and used the time to study the Greek some more. He was undeniably handsome in a glossy sort of way: very easy on the eye – and the ear, come to that. His views were clearly civilised; she trusted Gwyneth enough not to have picked him otherwise. Leontios was watching her assess him, and there was something else in his eyes. Catrina was not immediately sure what it was, but it made her pause mid sip.

'Of course not. How could I disapprove? Anyway, it's none of my business.'

'You could, easily,' Leontios retorted. 'It's good that you don't, though, because you may be seeing a lot of me while you are working with Gwyneth.'

They finished lunch, their conviviality warmed by the wine, and the engaged pair went off arm in arm to a Green group meeting. Catrina wondered what it was that had made her catch her breath while she had been watching the suave Leontios. Was it challenge – and was that a challenge to find fault, or something else? A challenge to find him attractive too? She must have misread the situation. Unless he automatically expected any woman to find him irresistible, which was quite possible, he had no reason to give her that message. And if any woman did fall for him, why had he picked the nondescript Gwyneth, who was many things but hardly a trophy?

She was still thinking about the look early that evening when, after an uneventful afternoon in the office, she went across to Café Franck to meet Patrice at the end of his shift.

Initially there was no sign of him so, needing to top up after drinking at lunchtime or risk an early hangover, Catrina ordered a gin and tonic from Damien and found a corner table while she waited for Patrice to emerge. He was, she assumed, in the back office finishing off the paperwork from the shift. She sat down and surveyed the room. There was no one she knew in sight, but that was not a surprise. Mercedes and her new friend, the Scottish Rory, would by now have delivered Fidel to Elise in Bolzano and Esko would be still working over at Parliament. There was an uncharitable measure of relief that Mariana was nowhere to be seen either. Catrina slugged back more than half of her G&T then lounged on the cushioned bench for a moment and closed her eyes.

'You look so comfortable my dear – just like a tabby cat.' The unmistakeable Russian accent of Nikita jolted her back to attention.

Catrina blinked. 'I am.'

'Then I shall get myself a drink and join you. That is a gin, you drink, I think? You might imagine I would drink vodka, but not here – not the way they do it in the West. I agree with you that here gin is the thing.' She dropped her mink coat on the bench by Catrina and swept to the bar.

By the time she had returned Catrina had finished her own drink and spotted Patrice emerging from the back office. 'Actually, I think I'll have another,' she announced.

'Oh my dear, how thoughtless of me. I should have asked,' Nikita berated herself as she sat down.

'That's all right. I can get my own. Don't worry.'

Although she covered the space between her and Patrice she found she was not the only one to waylay him. Agnestina, who had been so helpful with Esko's travel problems the previous day, was there first. That was OK; Catrina wanted a drink and just smiled at Patrice as she went around him to the counter. While she was waiting for the gin to arrive, though, she glanced back at him. Agnestina was asking something – she couldn't catch what in the idiomatic French. Her stomach leapt.

The look, though – the look that she was giving Patrice was exactly the same as Leontios had aimed at her. She placed it. It was the look a cat gives to anybody coming into a room: territorial, possessive, daring you to disagree and face the consequences.

IV

Tuesday

Trials with Four Legs

On Tuesday morning, soon after the obligatory dry roll and coffee had been brought round, Fidel was told by an exhausted junior doctor that he was free to leave hospital. He did not feel free at all. Although X-rays had proved that his right ankle was not broken but only badly sprained, as far as Fidel was concerned it made no difference. He was still heavily bandaged and in a great deal of pain. The wound had swollen nicely in the hours after he fell, and it showed little intention of going back to normal. Besides which, he had been told firmly not to put any weight on it for at least ten days.

Crutches had been issued, for a fee, almost as standard issue to anyone being discharged from Bolzano's thriving hospital in the wintertime, but if Fidel was no expert at staying on his own feet, on crutches he was hopeless. He sat on the edge of the bed in which he had spent the night 'under observation' and wondered mournfully how he was going to cope. After all, he was only here at all because he needed to see Elise. The world of comfortable social punditry and gently acid discourse which was his life in Brussels suddenly seemed a luxurious and irretrievable dream.

Slowly, timorously, he placed his good foot on the floor, grasped the handles of the crutches and tried to stand. Not much happened. Fidel's back and biceps had never been examples of athletic greatness, but now their failure was abject. If he could not even push off from the bed what hope was there?

Fidel sighed and tried again. The crutches slid away from under him as if they were on rollers and he only just managed to throw himself backwards on to the bed instead of crashing to the floor. He lay, crutches in hand, staring at the ceiling, and wondered if it was possible to make an even greater fool of himself than he was doing at the moment. Thank the Lord none of his students, let alone his so-called colleagues at the university, could see him. At least he didn't have to put up with their schadenfreude. Or not yet, anyway, he thought grimly.

Still, it had to be done. He sat up, once more planted the end of the crutches either side of him and pushed. It was as if someone had pressed the propel button. He rose without effort and stood. It was not all his own work, he realised quickly. His arms had been grabbed beneath the shoulder and lifted, doubling his upward force: a pair of rocket thrusters.

Fidel coyly looked to his left. There, grinning, was Mercedes' Scottish friend Rory, and a cautious glance told him that it was Mercedes herself reinforcing his right arm.

'Take a bit of getting used to, these things, but you'll soon get the hang of them,' Rory announced sympathetically.

Fidel was not so sure. He pressed down on his left foot, careful not to rest on his useless right, and gingerly brought his crutches a little way in front of him.

'That's the way,' Rory encouraged him. 'Small steps. Nothing too ambitious.'

Ambition was one thing that could not be further from his mind, he thought ruefully, but just managed a grumbled 'thank you' as the first two paces were accomplished.

'We thought we would take you along to Elise,' Mercedes smiled. 'She's awake and has been asking about you.'

Progress along the corridor to the lift, and then to the secluded area two floors above where Elise lay in a special room for those in a serious condition, was slow and, for Fidel, excruciating – not so much because of pain but more from the embarrassment of failing to master his crutches and the constant need for Rory and Mercedes to gather him before he tumbled. All independence had vanished.

Elise herself was sitting up in bed and, though still plugged into a succession of monitors and drips, was looking a lot better than the sorry semi-conscious wreck of the evening before. This time it was Fidel who looked pathetic, and when he appeared in the doorway, manoeuvring through with his two supporters, Elise greeted him with a brief shriek of laughter, her fractured ribs quickly reminding her that laughing was not such a good idea. The grin remained, though, as Fidel flopped gratefully on to a chair at her bedside.

'Oh, Fidel – you didn't have to!'

'Have to what?'

'Hurt yourself so badly just to make me feel better.'

'But I didn't intend—'

'Of course you did, don't be so modest. It was so thoughtful of you!'

Fidel was not used to being teased, but the idea that he was in fact in complete control of his predicament appealed to his sense of manhood, even if the crutches gave the lie. Sitting down, though, he could imagine such a motive.

'I did not really think about it,' he admitted, 'but when I fell and was lying on the ice and snow, I could at least imagine how you must have felt, my dear.'

In fact, Elise had no recollection at all of how she had felt in the snow. She had been out cold (literally) most of the time, and shock had conveniently wiped away what little memory of the accident remained. She looked up at Mercedes with the laughter still in her eyes. 'He's so sweet, isn't he.'

'Oh yes, and you know he really has made a mess of himself. He cannot put any weight on his ankle for ten days. It's so lucky Nikita has insisted we stay until Monday, but after that he will have to manage without us.'

'Imagine!' exclaimed Elise.

'I'm afraid I can,' Rory contributed. 'I don't think he will be able to lean on you too often.'

The horror of the position was beginning to dawn on Fidel even if the others were treating it as a huge joke at his expense. How would he and Elise get back to Brussels and deal with the stairs up to their flats, the steep slope of the road outside, the little challenges of everyday life? And it was only Tuesday. The next few days suddenly seemed the easy ones, with Mercedes and Rory in charge, bills paid by Nikita and the hospital to fall back on. When Elise's brother appeared in the room even the sacrifice of coming all the way to Italy seemed unnecessary.

Fidel could have cried. Instead he clasped Elise's hand and with great dignity smiled. 'What adventures we have.'

Saskia Disdains

'Tyron Wangstrutt at your service, ma'am.'

'I doubt it.'

The American, all big smile and handshake, was momentarily thunderstruck by the chill of the reply, but then he had not met Saskia before.

'Van Katwijk,' she continued. 'We will establish whether I am of service to you or not.'

'I'm sure you will, ma'am.'

TW, as he liked his friends to call him, was used to his name being a source of mirth in Europe – which, if not guaranteeing serious attention, at least elicited a degree of condescending amiability. Yet here he was, trailing behind this ferocious Dutch woman who could hardly have exhibited her indifference more clearly. He was ushered not to a secluded meeting room to *rendez-vous* (TW had practised his French) with a notable member of the Digital Security Committee, but to the very public coffee bar on the Parliamentary concourse – the same spot, as it happens, where Catrina had asked for a job with Gwyneth Price a few months before.

It became clear, too, that he was expected to buy the coffee. TW was already aware that the Belgian idea of coffee was a meagre half cup, about a seventh of the size he would have picked up stateside, and that it cost twice as much.

Ms van Katwijk, as TW was forced to call her since she had not vouchsafed a personal name, jostled her way to a free table in a distant recess and checked her email on her phone as she waited for him. When he eventually appeared, still smiling, with the coffee she was deep in conversation in Dutch, and showed no inclination to cease. TW wondered who was ruder – this creature, who was called an assistant, or the man who had served him the coffee without a word, as though the English language was foreign muck.

He had finished his pathetic cup by the time Saskia dragged her attention back to him.

'I am afraid my Member has been called back to Den Haag on urgent party business,' she began, 'so he cannot be available today. However, given the nature of the DSC's investigation into Ziggie Industries' monopolistic tendencies he would not have felt it appropriate to see you himself at this stage. We have lobbying rules these days, you know.'

'So I hear,' TW muttered, but then recovered himself. Time to keep the energy up, he told himself, and beamed. 'Oh sure, Ms van Katwijk – or may I call you—?'

'No.'

'Great. No impropriety on my part, I can assure you. None intended by Ziggie, either. I – we – thought it might be useful to touch base and, er, see how the land lies.'

'The land,' Saskia eyed him with the disdain of a lynx offered a vegan stew, 'is flat, but for you covered in substantial obstacles. And I never touch base.'

It took a lot to deflate Tyron Wangstrutt, but he had to admit that he could feel the air starting to leak out.

Saskia was peering at him with new derision. 'Were your family originally part of the Overijssel Wangstrutts?'

'I'm not rightly sure, ma'am, but I know they had Dutch connections back in the 1840s.' Maybe this could lighten her up – like asking the Brits if they knew Binns Minor at school.

'You should check,' advised Saskia. 'It could save you some trouble. Your company might think it wiser to appoint a different lobbyist.'

TW wondered what his ancestors could have done to so invoke the wrath of contemporary Europe that Ziggie Industries would have to chuck him. His brow furrowed – a rare occurrence for this most optimistic of corporate actors. Saskia had that effect on most people. TW was truly puzzled. The Wangstrutts had wandered west in the 1840s: well over a hundred and fifty years ago. Ancient history – as ancient for a good US citizen as the War of Spanish Succession for a European – yet here it was being invoked as a personal and national insult by a woman in her twenties.

'You want to give me a lead here, ma'am? Because where I come from the Wangstrutts are proud and solid citizens and—'

'Wangstrutt! Thought I'd find you around somewhere.'

TW jumped and looked round. For a moment the thought struck him that the Katwijk woman had edged him into this corner while she summoned the Parliamentary Police. But the face that accompanied the slap on the back was grinning.

'Ah, right, Bruno,' TW gasped in relief. 'Great.'

Saskia looked at Bruno the way a passionate gardener looks at a slug. She had seen him around – but then she had seen most people around, without being interested in who they were. At this moment he looked like providing the American with an excuse, and she realised she had been amused by his consternation. It was the only thing that had amused her that day.

'Hi – sorry to interrupt,' Bruno said, and glanced across to Saskia. 'I'm in Sanderson's office,' he explained. Saskia sniffed.

'So.' It was a statement, not even a rude question.

'Tyron, old son, I know I told you yesterday that the boss was busy and was likely to be for ever, but it seems I was jumping the gun.'

'Well, now, that is fine news. He got a time for me?'

'Now – if you're finished with…?'

'Miss van Katwijk,' TW supplied, 'and I guess she's finished with me – at least that is my impression.'

Saskia shrugged, implying that she didn't care whether she had on not.

'Not here, though,' Bruno continued. 'Early lunch, if you don't mind. Tony… Mr Sanderson can't stand this building. We'll find him out the back. Nice café in Place Luxembourg.'

'No problem. We Yanks usually do lunch earlier than you guys anyway.'

TW rose and nodded at Saskia. 'Nice to meet you, ma'am. Another time, maybe.'

The look he was wordlessly given in return made that an unlikely result – almost as unlikely as Ziggie Industries getting its way with the European Commission. Bruno took his turn to aim a half smile at Saskia. Quite pretty in a butch sort of way, he thought.

Saskia thought it unnecessary to take any view of Bruno whatever.

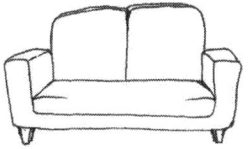

Taking a Seat

Mariana looked up in undisguised surprise when Catrina walked into her office just as she was tidying the desk before heading down to the cafeteria.

'Can I help you?' she asked stiffly.

'I doubt it,' Catrina answered, perhaps a little too truthfully. 'I've come to see Esko. He asked me to.'

'Oh?' Mariana's surprise evolved into suspicion. 'What about?'

Catrina suddenly didn't want to tell Mariana. It was not fair or logical, but if she had analysed it she would have said that any woman who could show interest in the rat Bruno did not have judgement that could be trusted. That this applied equally to herself was, of course, beside the point.

'Nothing much. Esko was there on Sunday when some friends were organising a visit to another one who'd had an accident. He asked me to drop by and update him.'

The look Mariana gave her suggested that the tale was unlikely.

'Well, he's in there,' Mariana nodded with diminishing interest to the internal door, then, as Catrina made to walk away, called her back. 'I'm sorry,' she began.

Catrina stopped and gazed at her in puzzlement. 'What for?'

'For being so rude on Sunday – about Bruno. When you told me what he was like.'

'No, you weren't rude. I was,' said Catrina, softening immediately. 'It was none of my business. It was just a bit of a surprise, that's all.'

'But you were right. Completely right. Only a few minutes later he said things about art, and that gallery near Flagey… Its owner…'

'Nikita.'

'Yes, the Russian. I realised what he was really like. How could I have been so stupid?'

Catrina shrugged. 'So was I, in September, only it took me weeks to get out of it. At least you realised after a few days.'

'Still…'

'Yes, he's a slug – and a thick slug at that.'

'The thing is, it's so hard.'

'What is?'

Mariana swallowed and wondered whether it was a good idea to go on. Catrina had, in her experience, never shown a great propensity for being sympathetic. 'Finding a man who is not.'

'A slug? Oh, I don't know,' she said, and nodded at the room next door. 'Esko seems OK.'

She could not have known, but she could hardly have said anything less sensitive to Mariana. The Finn pursed her lips and returned her gaze to the computer. Catrina was dismissed, though since she was already through and closing the door to Esko's inner office, her dismissal went unnoticed.

Esko looked up and smiled. 'Hi, sit down. Forgive me while I just finish this email.'

Catrina smiled back and wondered which of the seats to take. Either of the chairs in front of the desk would surely make this a political business meeting. Maybe she should take the couch, but that might imply a familiarity which she, a mere Parliamentary Assistant, could not assume, especially with a group leader. Esko saved her the decision by looking up again and waving at the couch.

Comfy, then. Catrina relaxed.

Esko tapped away at the keyboard, read back the message, clicked send, thought with his brow lightly furrowed for a minute, then came round to the front of the desk, swivelled a chair and sat, the furrows banished and a smile in place. Definitely not a slug, Catrina thought to herself, but equally definitely a politician – a quality she had never been conscious of in the bar at Flagey, where he had been thought of mainly as Amelie's boyfriend, but was far more aware of in Esko's own territory.

'Are you really going on this mad trip to Bolzano?' he began.

'I don't know. I haven't really thought about it,' Catrina admitted. 'I suppose I should.'

'Think about it or go?'

'Maybe both. Are you going?'

Esko paused, wondering how much he could trust Catrina not to gossip. Take the risk.

'It's tempting but complicated. If I go south I would have to visit Amelie in France as well. I think she would be pleased, but then, surprising an actress on location – not always a good idea. She might be happier imagining me having a dull weekend in Brussels.'

'Really?'

'Who knows,' Esko shrugged. 'Then there are other complications. I could not go as Nikita's guest. She is Russian, even if she is well established here, and accepting hospitality like that would have to be declared as a gift. I am from Finland – even more difficult. And then I would be visiting Italy where Roberto, my predecessor at SLEE, is fighting charges of false expenses. So you see, it is not as simple as for you.'

'So you are not coming.'

'I didn't say that, quite. I said it was not simple. On the other hand, if Amelie is free to join me for a little skiing – it is always good for a Finn to be seen on skis – and everybody knows I am paying for myself, then it will make the newspapers, and there will be a contrast between the old "expenses-paid" leader and the new one, transparently taking his glamorous lady for a romantic weekend in the mountains, while doing the decent thing and going to see a friend who has had an accident.'

'Gosh,' said Catrina, immediately glad she was not a politician.

'So, what about you?'

'I can get away on Friday, and probably Gwyneth won't need me much on Monday. And Nikita is very insistent, of course, and I've never been to the Dolomites.'

'All good reasons,' urged Esko.

'But then, if Patrice can't come and you and Amelie don't, I would be getting in the way of Mercedes and her Rory and have to go everywhere with Nikita,' Catrina reasoned, tying herself in her usual knots, 'and I've never been skiing in my life, so I'd probably end up in the same room as Elise.'

'Or Fidel,' Esko laughed. The text from Mercedes about Fidel's literal downfall had done the rounds, complete with photos.

'Don't!'

'Perhaps we should not decide now, after all. Maybe I should talk to Amelie and you to Patrice. What's your number?' Catrina gave it to him and he tapped it into his phone. 'Fine – I'll text you this evening.'

So that was that, thought Catrina as she made her way back to her own office, changing her mind halfway and heading for lunch feeling as though the working year was starting with more tangles than she was ready to untie. Rather like her hairy Afghan bag, really.

V

Wednesday

A Journalist's Insecurity

In Bolzano Wednesday was starting with rain, the steady implacable rain that falls from unbroken cloud with no intention of shifting for a week if it can help it. A hundred metres up the slopes of the mountains the cloud was discretely laying down a blanket of snow under cover that would thrill the skiers when the sun eventually pushed away the gloom. For Wednesday, though, the Bolzano pavements were latrines of slush and the mountains might not have existed.

Rory sat in a café and sipped at his third macchiato of the morning while scrolling with ebbing interest through the news sites on his laptop. Mercedes was attending to Fidel and getting him into a fit state to visit Elise again, still firmly under observation three days after her calamitous fall. There was no hurry. The doctors would be making their rounds and Elise's brother was in theory on hand to try and prise some conclusions out of them. For a few hours at least Rory was not needed.

Looking out of the window did nothing to cheer him. With weather like this he might as well have been in Huddersfield. He grimaced at the thought, then smiled. No – the coffee would not have been as good, nor the pastries, especially the little ones full of freshly made sweet custard – so delicious. Bolzano in the rain was still better than anywhere northern – even Brussels, which caught the rain more than most places.

That he was there at all was bothering Rory, however. Why had it been so easy to get permission to disappear for another week after New Year? In theory the political world was waking up. By Friday surely somebody in Brussels would be worth a story? The season of speculative think pieces on the shape of the world to come should have given way to the first gory stories of what had gone wrong while everyone had been in holiday denial. The excuse he had given Mercedes – that nobody had recovered from New Year enough to want real political news – was only half true. News was news, whenever it happened.

There had been rumours before that his paper, *Europe Now*, the only English-language weekly covering the European space (as it sententiously described itself) was losing the will to print – that the owners, a multimedia group in London not known for its patience, were getting bored and, worse, were less than impressed with the advertising figures. The online-only ghetto beckoned: not much better than being a blogger.

WEDNESDAY

Talk was gathering that real paid journalists would be winkled out and replaced with random snippets from the web assembled by a subeditor who would be more techno-freak than writer. Rory could feel his job slipping away just as he was settling into Brussels and, more importantly, Mercedes' life.

In a surge of paranoia he typed in the web address of his paper and scanned the columns for clues. His name was still in the contributing editors' section, so that was something. He had not been sacked while he was on the train. Nonetheless Bolzano was unlikely to be the setting for a juicy story unless someone blew up a mountain as part of a regional-development scam and in the January rain Rory thought it might not be such a bad idea anyway. He sighed and wondered if his nerves could stand more coffee.

Across the Via Laurino from the café in which Rory was massaging his worries stood one of the grander hotels that graced the city – one that was aimed at those with an appreciation of elegant city life, not puddles of water from sodden ski clothes. Rory glanced up as the flashing blue lights of the police escort for a three-car motorcade (one police Fiat leading two shiny black limos) drew up at the hotel entrance.

In Brussels he would hardly have bothered to look: the city was so infested with political dignitaries every day that sometimes motorcades felt like the only traffic. In Bolzano, though, Rory suspected it was more of a rarity, and the journalist in him who never truly took time off watched with professional curiosity as young men in smart grey suits exposed the fancy cloth to the rain. They climbed from front seats and whisked out umbrellas ready to shield their VIP cargo from the elements.

The VIP paused under his shelter as a distinguished-looking man, presumably the manager, demonstrated his subservient status by rushing forward in greeting without guarding against the deluge. The VIP shook the proffered hand, ran fingers through his mop of slightly too black hair and looked up and down the street as if expecting a crowd that had inexplicably failed to turn up.

Rory frowned as he watched the performance. There was something about the man that he recognised: clearly not the unlamented former Italian Prime Minister – too young and the hair was nearly natural – but of that ilk. And something nudged the back of his mind – a hunch that he should be surprised to see that particular personage in Bolzano on a wet Wednesday in January. He pulled out his phone and snapped a picture before the man turned away and strode into the hotel.

His paper was still just about solvent enough to employ a picture editor. It was a long shot but... Rory forwarded the photo.

Any idea who this is?

A minute or so later the phone buzzed.

Not sure – give me 5.

That was excuse enough to justify the extra coffee. He had barely had time to get back to his table by the window when another limousine drew up, but without the benefit of flashing lights. Rory's interest was firmly caught by now, and this time he had no difficulty recognising the quietly fashionable woman in her late forties as she was greeted in turn by the manager (who had remembered an umbrella this time). Lucia Redetti, Italy's member of the European Commission, who had been given the unenviable portfolio of Regional Affairs. Rory knew that she was Venetian, so popping up the autostrada for a spot of winter sports was a possibility, but she was not unloading cases. There needed to be an explanation.

Only one way to find out, Rory thought to himself, shutting down his laptop and slipping it into his tatty canvas bag. He draped his anorak over his head for the dash across the street.

Cognac in the Morning

In Flagey the Café Franck was quieter than usual. Snow lay thick on the ground outside and the swept pavements were lethal skating rinks – no better than in Bolzano. The trams forging their way around the square were ice-breakers, wheels crunching through the layers that filled the tracks. The sun was making valiant attempts to come out over the frozen lake, but a thin veil of cloud persisted, as if guarding the winter's modesty, and little perceptible warmth came with the light. It was not a morning to sally out unless you had to, and most of those not working took the hint.

An exception was Nikita. This weather reminded her so strongly of St Petersburg that she embraced it happily

– mostly because it gave her the chance to flaunt her furs, especially her sable hat, in which she knew she looked stunning – nothing like the twenty-somethings that draped themselves across modern Russian magazines but, Nikita liked to think, as she piled her blonde hair underneath, maybe with just a touch of Julie Christie from *Doctor Zhivago*, that most romantic of films that was still banned at home when she was a little girl. It was sad that only old ladies wore hats indoors these days, she reflected, as she laid hers reverently on the spare chair next to her in Café Franck just before half-past eleven that Wednesday morning.

For once she was glad there was no service at tables. It meant that delicious young barman – the one who was so unaccountably attached to dowdy little Catrina – had been treated to the full-fur experience as she ordered her black coffee and a little refresher of cognac. She had even lured him into stroking the hat itself. Such little triumphs made a morning.

In truth Nikita was feeling a trifle spare. The gallery was closed and, rather to her surprise, she was missing the bubbly but sensible presence of Mercedes, who had become a welcome foil for her own exuberance, alternating with dramatic gloom, over the months. Nikita was quietly sure that having to open the gallery in the morning for Mercedes had saved her from Father's solution to oncoming winter – breakfast vodka.

There was no man in her life, she reflected, looking rather wistfully across at Patrice. He was years younger, but maybe that was what she needed. Her strategy had been to look a few years older than she really was, hoping to forestall men who wanted to marry her and beget children (in which she was profoundly uninterested, happy to be nice to other people's babies without having to actually pick the little horrors up). Now, though, there was a string of elderly diplomats and Commission officials at her door, delighted by the exotic and sophisticated fortyish woman in her cutting edge gallery. However, the forty-something would only actually turn thirty-eight in March, and a dalliance from within her own decade felt in order.

Nikita gave her coffee a sour look and unconsciously adjusted the shoulder strap of her bra. The pre-lunch prospects in the Café Franck did not look promising. Maybe she could attract with more success in Italy over the weekend. There, her style and furs would be more appreciated than in the eclectic melting pot of Ixelles.

Her attention turned to the practicalities of the weekend. She had blithely invited half Brussels to Bolzano, it seemed. She was not much worried by the cost – she could charm one of those same elderly diplomats into buying a picture he might, and his wife certainly not, want. Who was coming, though? Mercedes and her Scottish boy were already there, along with that apology for a professor, but what of the rest? She dialled Mercedes.

'Darling!'

'Hi Nikita,' she answered, with rather less enthusiasm. Mercedes was not unhappy to hear from her employer. It was just that, at that moment, she had just walked out of the door after escorting Fidel to Elise's bedside, and was trying to negotiate opening her inadequate pocket umbrella while avoiding the little lakes of freezing water trapped between the mounds of slush.

'You don't sound very happy.'

'I'm fine, it's just… Could I call you back in ten minutes when I am out of the rain?'

'Rain! But you are in the mountains.'

'Where it is raining – and you cannot see the mountains. Talk to you soon.' Mercedes rang off.

Nikita looked at her silent phone and slumped back. She sighed and sipped the final dregs of her cognac.

Her jaunt to the Dolomites began to feel less attractive. She had been thinking of *vino caldo* after a long afternoon admiring the peaks from a horse-drawn sleigh; some of those lovely Italian aperitivi before dinner. And then she remembered that Bolzano was also dual-language, rather too Germanic Bolzen, and the glamour started to shrink. The alternative, though, was to sit tight in Brussels, and that did not hold much promise either.

Deflated, she decided another cognac might help, although it was really dangerously early. Still, Frenchmen did it all the time. Why should not a Russian woman? She sauntered back to the bar, keen not to look too desperate.

'Another?' asked Patrice with understanding in his smile.

'If you'd be so kind,' she said, feeling instantly coquettish. Patrice nodded and obliged. The mobile phone in her bag warbled its tone – the opening bars of Mussorgsky's *Pictures at an Exhibition*, which had seemed a terribly clever idea for the Russian gallery owner at the time, but which was now as tiresome to her as everybody else.

'Mercedes, are you dry now, darling?' she said, loud enough for Patrice to hear.

'All except my feet.'

'And how is our patient?'

'You mean patients – I have two of them now.'

'Yes, so you do.' Nikita caught Patrice's eye. 'Tell me in a minute. I'm in the café. I think Patrice wants to hear first.' She handed over the phone.

'Hallo? Yes, how are they? Oh. I see. Tell them we all miss them, will you? And you, of course. My love to Elise. It is very sad. Tell her we need her back soon.' He gave the phone to its owner again and topped up the cognac.

'Well?' Nikita barked across the continent.

There was a sigh at the other end. 'You are coming?' Mercedes asked in return.

'Yes, maybe Friday'.

'I should check flights if you can. It may be hard to get one then. I can book you a room here, but there are nicer hotels. We were trying not to cost you too much.'

Nikita honestly had never thought about this. There was going to have to be an afternoon of research.

Elise Begins to Function

On the fourth day after her parting at speed from the snowboard, Elise was beginning to take the hint from her body that recovery from this was going to take longer than losing a hangover. Nonetheless the doctor on her morning round explained that there was good reason for optimism. The concussion she had suffered when head had met rock was not as severe as originally feared. The brain had not swelled beyond manageable proportions. Meanwhile...

Meanwhile, thought Elise, drifting away from the doctor's thick accent, everything hurt. The morphine drip was under her own control now – she could dose herself whenever the pain became too dominant – but although the drug lifted her above the pain she knew it was still there. For the first time she could isolate the damaged places, locating agony centres instead of a sense of general awfulness. Her pelvis and left knee seemed most messed up, and her right wrist felt as though it had been broken off and then put back together with a bit of old sticky tape (which, had she known, just about summed up the reality). She must have bruised badly, if not fully broken, her ribcage in the fall, judging by the way her lungs protested whenever she breathed in – and then there was the headache: full, rich and relentless.

Into this miasma of hurt hobbled the wounded Fidel, starting to co-ordinate his crutches at last, if not ready to forgo the reassuring arm of Mercedes as he struggled to Elise's bedside. Elise smiled a weak good morning as Fidel leant over to kiss her, but to go with her own pain there was a pang of guilt at his. Only because she had been thoughtless enough to fall and demand that he come to rescue her was he now so helpless himself.

Behind Fidel and Mercedes the nurse hovered, eager to take readings before Elise was allowed to socialise. And behind her still another figure hovered, bearing flowers.

'You are popular this morning,' observed the nurse, but continued to note down figures on her chart as the machines delivered the body's secrets. 'I will not be long, but neither must your friends. We need you to rest more than talk.'

Elise, reaching over to press the morphine button, agreed with her, but was determined not to show it. 'He is not my friend, he is my brother,' she said, not meaning any unkindness in the distinction.

The young man, a remarkable contrast to his sister, stepped forward. Where she was elfin and slight, he was tall and broad with the shoulders of a rugby player, at nineteen sporting patchy stubble as the start of a ginger beard. He handed the flowers to the nurse and took his sister's hand. 'Better?'

'Maybe a little,' Elise tried to assure him. 'Fidel, Mercedes, this is Artur.'

'We saw him yesterday,' smiled Mercedes, 'when we were leaving. We didn't really meet, though. You were not aware enough to introduce us.'

Artur was peered at and appraised, very favourably by Mercedes, with a touch of trepidation by Fidel who, to his credit, abandoned his persona of second victim and turned as swiftly as he could to take the young man's hand with the confidence of a man in control. It didn't fool the women, but then it was not meant to. The bravura signalled that Fidel might be nearly three times Artur's age and minus the use of one ankle, but he was still Elise's lover and worthy of respect.

Artur disarmed him with a grin. 'Of course, I have heard so much. It was incredible you came so fast, so quickly.'

A deprecating hand was waved by Fidel. 'How could I not? Elise is…' he struggled for a word which did her justice. Surely his eloquence had not deserted him along with his balance? He waved his hand at her. 'Everything,' he finished lamely.

It seemed to delight Artur, however. 'But you are right. She is everything, to me, to us,' he moved over to kiss his sister on the forehead. 'I always knew that, naturally. Until Sunday, though I had no idea what that really meant, then she could have just…' – the young man clung to Elise's fingers – '…just gone.'

To his surprise Fidel found himself grasping Artur by the shoulder in comfort. 'I know. Impossible!'

'Yes, well, I am still here,' announced Elise, secretly pleased at the exhibition of affection, but also just a little annoyed that her two men were speaking about her in the third person.

Mercedes had watched the meeting of Artur and Fidel with interest; young brother, older lover could have been tense, but already they seemed to be the best of friends. She looked at her phone and read a text from Rory. 'On a story, I think. Come to big hotel on Via Laurino. Need you for cover.'

She sniffed. Just for cover! Typical. Nonetheless, she had done her duty at the hospital. 'Artur, will you be able to help the professor home? I need to meet my friend.'

'Of course. I will be happy to.'

A puzzled frown formed on Elise's face. It was the first morning after her operation that she was fully aware of her surroundings. 'But Mercedes, I don't understand. What are you doing here? My brother was with me, and I hoped Fidel would come – but you?'

'It's a little complicated,' Mercedes admitted. 'When we heard the news on Sunday we were all together in Flagey. Patrice, Catrina and a nice French girl whose name I can't remember helped plan Fidel's travel, but it was so difficult Nikita thought I and my new friend Rory should come with him. I'm very glad. She was right.'

Elise looked at Fidel's ankle, laughed and regretted it as her ribs tightened. 'Yes, she was. But the cost!'

'Oh, you know Nikita. She likes the grand gesture – and a few expenses for the gallery. She is talking about coming herself tomorrow and bringing Catrina and Patrice with her.'

'Oh.' A party at her bedside was not Elise's idea of recovery. She would have to have a little relapse, perhaps.

Pending Questions

In Brussels many things that had been unclear on Tuesday afternoon had become much clearer by Wednesday morning. There was the political conundrum of whether Esko should join the gathering in Bolzano and whether Amelie would appear with him. The answer was not immediately straightforward. Esko's first question, when he had eventually managed to get his actress to pick up the call on his fourth attempt (and then had to repeat everything as Amelie struggled to hear in the hubbub of a Provençal bistro) had been whether he should join her for the weekend. Amelie was surprised, and tried to sound delighted, but Esko knew her too well not to recognise when it was the actress speaking, not his lover.

Instead of pressing the point, he rephrased the question. If she was being an actress he would be a politician, and make a note to come back to winkling out the reason for her reluctance later. 'How about joining me for a little skiing – but not in France, across in Italy: Bolzano?'

Still Amelie was wary. 'Why Bolzano?' She was told a very edited version of the Elise story, since her concentration was clearly on fruits de mer rather than the sound of Esko's voice.

Somewhere about the account of Fidel slipping and Mercedes taking charge, Amelie interrupted. 'But that's a wonderful idea! I can get away Friday morning, probably even tomorrow night. I shall have to stop in Milan, of course – do some shopping. I have nothing to wear for the mountains.'

Esko gave silent thanks that he would probably miss that bit.

Amelie had different ideas. 'You could fly in and meet me there – or even here in Provence. You never need to be in Brussels on Fridays.'

'I'm sure I could,' he murmured softly. MEPs in Finland were paid well, and as a Group Leader he had a supplement, but he was wondering already whether having a film star deciding his shopping habits was going to be more than his credit card could chew. After the call he thought about asking Mariana to book the flight and hotel, but then realised that it would be unfair and, if he was to make the point about the difference between public and private in a MEP's affairs, none of her business. He resigned himself to an hour online in his flat.

While Esko grappled with travel sites from FlyLow to BedRight, Nikita, Catrina and Patrice had settled down at a corner table in Café Franck and had been joined by Agnestina, who was repeating her laptop travel-agent service of Sunday afternoon. She was amazed, though, when as she was about to push the button and book the flights Nikita put a hand on her arm.

'My dear, you've forgotten someone.'

'Who?' Agnestina looked around her in bafflement.

'You, of course. You've done all this work. Of course you must come. It will do you good and, you know, it will be nice to have another woman without a man along. You don't have one at the moment, do you?'

'I suppose not,' the beautiful French girl admitted, catching Patrice's inquisitive glance and suddenly realising that she had neither heard from, nor thought much about, Flamand since before Christmas, except when she had explained his ejection to Patrice.

'There you are, then. That's settled,' announced Nikita. Catrina felt a shudder. She couldn't tell why.

Tyron Wangstrutt had retreated to his hotel by taxi in the middle of Tuesday afternoon, having drunk more average wine with Bruno's MEP, Tony Sanderson, than he had ever thought possible at lunchtime. The MEP had returned from the café in Place Luxembourg to his duties in Parliament apparently unaffected. TW realised as soon as he stood up that he was profoundly affected. As a corporate fixer and lobbying great in the bars and restaurants of Washington, DC, TW knew that there were few who could match his capacity for night-time bourbon. But this European thing was different. In Washington you could be having a working breakfast with endless coffee almost as soon as dawn broke at six. Lunch would happen at midday and water or some variety of fizzy drink with no kick was now the politically respectable norm.

Brussels, though, ran on beer and wine. Nobody thought twice about a beer or a *pichet* to start the day, and lunch without at least *un demi* each was unthinkable. Even so, TW must have gone the full litre and then some.

He went to bed as darkness fell at five. At ten he woke still drunk and yet with a head that pounded and stabbed with the determination of a homicidal maniac. He had no idea where he was or why – all he knew was that the CIA waterboarding had clearly worked a treat. TW swallowed as many Tylenol as he thought his liver could stand and sank feverishly back to bed.

When Wednesday morning came TW wished profoundly that it had left him out of its plans. The headache was less vicious, it was true, but it had not retreated completely, hanging round the back of his skull just to remind him that it was ready to get active again whenever it felt the urge. Instead his stomach churned and TW could feel the ache in his joints and the thickening of his sinuses that told him a cold, flu even, was about to break into the open. His first act of the day was to sneeze and to carry on sneezing until he fell back exhausted.

He recovered enough to make it to the bathroom, use a dozen tissues and hurl himself under the healing pressure of a hot shower before, feeling ill but triumphant, ringing down to reception for a room-service breakfast, 'cooked, with nothing continental about it, and double coffee.'

The response was professional. 'Of course, monsieur, but since it is now after ten o'clock that will be the all-day breakfast, as I am sure monsieur understands. I suspect, however, that therefore monsieur will be unlikely to be able to vacate his room and check out by eleven, as in our conditions. Would monsieur be happy with an extra half hour? Any later than that and I am afraid we shall have to apply an extra charge of thirty per cent.'

TW struggled to compute. 'What do you mean, "vacate"? Do you mean I'm checking out?'

'That is the implication of your booking, monsieur.'

'But I'm here till Friday. I don't fly home till Friday – if not later. Probably next week.'

'That may be the case, monsieur, but your booking with us is until the 9th of January, and that is today.'

'Hell! That goddam intern. Never trust an intern, son, however goddam pretty.'

'I will listen to the advice, monsieur.'

'But I can stay, right? I mean, I can keep my room?'

'I regret not, monsieur. We are full for the next two nights. There is no possibility, unless there is a cancellation, but even so the room must be vacated.'

TW winced as some animal gripped his gall bladder between serrated teeth. 'Wonderful!'

There was a pause at the other end while the receptionist ordered the breakfast and let TW digest the news. 'However, monsieur, I have taken the liberty of anticipating this situation and, in view of monsieur's considerable patronage of our facilities over the last week I have enquired at both our near-adjacent hotels, and both will be able to accommodate you. I have reserved rooms. One has similar services to ours but is, how shall I say, a little more expensive.'

'How much?' Wangstrutt groaned.

'Approximately double.'

'Impossible.'

'Possible, though possibly not reasonable.'

'And the other?'

'Somewhat cheaper than us, monsieur, but I regret without a restaurant service and with rooms that are…' – he struggled for a suitably derogatory word – '…perhaps more commercial.'

'OK. Well thanks, son. I'll get some coffee in my system and let you know.'

Coffee as Disguise

In Bolzano, Rory had crossed the street from his café and settled himself into the lounge of the more luxurious hotel by the time his phone buzzed. His picture editor in Brussels had been almost as good as his word. It had taken him only ten minutes, not the promised five, to send a text identifying the slick man with a motorcade:

Think it's Borelli.

That didn't help Rory a great deal. His knowledge of Italian celebrity was mainly confined to football, and he was fairly certain no Borelli played for either AC or Inter Milan, or even Juve. He shrugged and thanked the stars for the modern joys of clever phones. He tapped in the name. 'Of course,' he muttered to himself as a waiter arrived at his chair and solicited an order. That was when he ordered coffee for two and called Mercedes back from the hospital to provide cover. Without her his lingering in the front foyer of the hotel would soon cause comment and, beyond that, likely eviction.

He settled back to read through the background on Borelli, who by this time had disappeared from view, along with his entourage and the Commissioner.

Alessandro Borelli, always known as Sanzo, was still in his mid-thirties, but making a noise in Italy – mainly in the north, but increasingly in Rome too. He had started his own party, and it was doing very well in the lower reaches of the River Po. His political thesis was simple: Italy had been a terrible mistake; Garibaldi had been nothing more than a pawn of the kings of Savoy. Most of all, it had meant the end of the Venetian Republic – for a thousand years the most adventurous, wealthy and democratic of all European states (and, thought Rory, some would say the most duplicitous, avaricious and exploitative too). The revival of the Venetian Republic was Borelli's mission – not as a right-wing populist franchise, but as a modern liberal mercantile state within the European Union, unfettered by the infighting in distant Rome – or the Mafia Papal States, as Borelli referred disparagingly to everywhere else in Italy. What caught Rory's eye, though, was Borelli's hitching of the Venetian call for secession to those of Scotland and Catalunya.

The coffee was taking an age to arrive – clearly the hotel had more important guests to cater for – but that suited Rory just fine. Mercedes arrived, though, sopping wet and feeling ill-used, just as the waiter returned with the tray, laden with dainty cups, silver pot and dinky pastries. If Rory had been trying to mollify his lady, he could not have timed it better. As the dripping outer clothes were discarded, and the waiter chivalrously wiped the water from her hands, Mercedes' scowl evaporated.

'This is nice,' she said, collapsing into the low cushions of the armchair.

Thank heavens for that, thought Rory.

'So what is the big mystery – what am I cover for?'

'Well, the cover is to explain why I am waiting for ever in the lobby with nowhere better to go. No manager will think twice about it if we are together. The mystery – I'm not quite sure yet, but I am convinced there is one.'

Mercedes looked underwhelmed, poured herself some coffee and slipped off her wet boots. 'It is big, then.'

Rory grinned. 'Huge. You know who Lucia Redetti is?'

'Not really. Let me guess – someone in Brussels.'

'Normally, yes. She is the Commissioner for Regional Affairs.' He could feel Mercedes' interest ebbing further and decided to make it more personal. 'Which means she's in charge of things like whether Catalunya would stay in the EU if it broke away from Spain, and whether people from Barcelona and Valencia – if it joined Greater Catalunya – would be still allowed to live in Brussels.'

'Oh!' Mercedes stopped rubbing her feet and suddenly gave Rory her full attention.

'She's here.'

'Here?'

'I've just seen her coming into the hotel.'

'Why shouldn't she – she's Italian?'

'There's more to it than that, I think.' Rory was warming to his tale. 'She came in just after Sanzo Borelli, the new whizz-kid who wants to re-invent the Venetian Republic and do the same as your lot and my lot: independence within the EU.'

'A very small republic,' sniffed the Catalunyan, who just as often thought of herself as Spanish when she thought about it at all. Maybe she needed to think about it more seriously. She hated decisions, especially political ones.

'It depends which Venice we are talking about – the city state in the lagoon, or the territory that covered all the flat lands around it and the northern coast of the Adriatic. I don't think he has the nerve, yet, to claim Istria, the Dalmatian and Greek coasts or all of Crete.'

'Sounds like a package-holiday company.'

'Very similar.'

Mercedes went back to massaging the damp and cold from her feet. 'Is it nice in this hotel?'

'I expect so. They make enough fuss.'

'Nice enough for Nikita?'

Rory looked around at the gilt mirrors, the ornate sideboards with their marble tops, the comfortable furniture modelled for an age when no traveller arrived without servants. 'You know her better than me, but if it's pampering she requires, I'm sure this place can do it.'

'Then I'll book her in.' Mercedes strode over to the reception desk while Rory sent a text about the likelihood of Borelli and Redetti having business together. The more he thought about it, the more unlikely it became. Redetti was also Venetian, but from a very different political background – an old-fashioned Italian socialist with a touch of the new pragmatism, as befitted someone faced with the realities of Brussels compromise. One thing was obvious, though – meeting in Venice itself would not have been an option for either of them.

Mercedes returned, smiling, talking into her phone with one hand and carrying a pair of hotel slippers in the other. She finished her call.

'And?' he enquired.

'She's in – and so are we! She says she doesn't want to be alone, so we are to move over here now. We get the extra night because they have a deal – five nights for the price of four. And I get my boots dried, so all you need to do is check out of ours and move the bags over.'

Rory shook his head. 'Oh no. I'm not moving from here until Redetti comes out.'

Mercedes looked at him with a mixture of fury and desperation. 'You want me to go out there again, with my feet still wet – just because you think some official might make a story?'

The Scotsman took her hand. 'No, I don't want that at all, but it is what is going to happen. Welcome to life with a journalist.'

Misery Compounded

Whoever said that Wednesday's child was a child of grief could have been thinking sympathetically of Tyron Wangstrutt as he grappled with the tripartite miseries of force-ten hangover, flu assault and the need to pack and find a new hotel room in under an hour. All his willpower was needed as he made 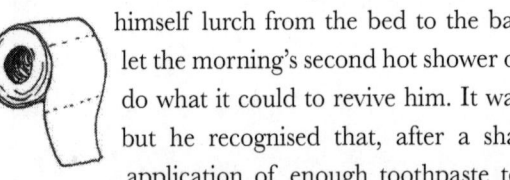 himself lurch from the bed to the bathroom and let the morning's second hot shower on full power do what it could to revive him. It was not much, but he recognised that, after a shave and the application of enough toothpaste to take away the taste of the rancid wine left over from Tuesday's lunch, he could just about contemplate moving around upright.

He had shirt and underpants on when a waitress appeared with his all-day breakfast. Neither were feeling up to being impressed with each other's extracurricular qualities. The food, once revealed from under its polished steel domes, was American style in theory, but with Belgian equivalents to the cream, fake maple syrup and buttermilk TW was used to. Real milk for his coffee, not boiled to death for shelf life, maple syrup that had even met maple trees and fresh rich cream served with Belgian *gaufres* made it a different culinary experience. The bacon was crisp but not incinerated, and had some meat, the coffee had only recently been roasted and ground, and came in a cafetière to be poured into a ceramic cup suitable for the strength of the brew, not as a volume of weak brown water in a cardboard container. Eggs were poached till their yolks were just turning firm and served over a brioche. Had TW been in less of a hurry and in better shape, he would have adored it.

Sadly, however, he was not in a condition to adore anything. The best he could manage was a grunt as the hot coffee hit his nervous system and the fats began to line his stomach. He ate half of what was on the tray then completed dressing, though a blotch of egg and a smear of creamy syrup meant the shirt would have to be changed again.

He was just pulling up his fly when his phone announced an incoming text and the room phone rang. The text from HQ at Ziggie Industries simply read:

Report progress soonest – especially expenses vs. outcome.

TW grimaced. It was 2 a.m. in Silicon Valley. Not fair.

'Yuh?' he growled into the phone.

'Monsieur Wanstroote…' began the unctuous voice of the man at reception.

'Wangstrutt,' he corrected.

'Monsieur?'

'The name is Wangstrutt, not Wanstroote.'

'*Oui, monsieur*. Whatever monsieur says. We are enquiring whether you will be leaving us soon, and whether you wish to take advantage of our other hotels?'

'Still no room, huh?'

'I am desolated, but no.'

'And still no deal on your other place like a big price downsize to same price as here?'

'I have tried, monsieur, but Brussels is very busy, and it is felt that a corporation such as yours will understand the pressures of competition.'

'Yeah – putting the screws on.' TW thought of his hangover, thought of spending an hour on travel sites for a reasonable price and thought most of the flu gaining ground. He needed comfort, sympathy and, above all, service. And screw California at 2 a.m.! 'OK – I'll take it till Monday. I'll reassess over the weekend.'

'Monsieur is very wise. While you will be paying a high price until Saturday, you will be relieved to know the weekend price does indeed fall considerably. I will send our porter to help with your bags in forty minutes?'

'Whatever.' TW put down the phone, sneezed and returned to the second half of his breakfast.

To be fair to TW (which he usually felt strongly the world was not), he was at the front desk checking out – and making sure the 'bar' bills were itemised on the receipt as 'restaurant' – five minutes before the smooth-tongued receptionist expected him. His body still felt as though he'd been purged by a basket of hot chillies then whipped by the Spanish Inquisition, but he was walking and presentable.

'So where is this other joint of yours?' enquired TW when the eye-watering account for drinks had been disguised and settled.

'Joint, monsieur? Ah, the Hotel Dutoit is situated a mere three hundred metres away, just by le Palais de Justice. You will find it very simply.' A map was produced with a flourish and marked.

'Find? You mean walk? You mean, no taxi?'

'It is so close, monsieur. Five minutes, maybe seven.'

'So?'

'And a taxi would have to go up to Defacz, then back down to Stephanie, then the wrong direction on the ring... I cannot get a taxi to agree to that.'

TW was not impressed. 'Yeah? Well, son, there's snow out there and I can.' He stalked out, dragging his bag, the other hand waving twenty euros.

Incredibly there was no taxi waiting outside to be bribed – and no doorman to summon one with a whistle and imperious salute. TW turned left, failing to see the grins on the faces of the hotel staff as he did so.

There were always taxis outside the grand establishment just down Avenue Louise – but not today. The motorcades of visiting ministers and a couple of protective army trucks had banished the taxis to the back entrance on Rue Charleroi, as TW discovered when he dragged his case down to the roundabout at Stephanie. There truly was nothing for it but to walk the last hundred and fifty metres, even if his feet were cold. At least the fresh freezing air had acted on his hangover like a dose of smelling salts.

The Hotel Dutoit was an ignoble tower on the fringe of the old inner city of Brussels, the heart of Belgium's government quarter, rather than the EU's. It exuded multinational five-star impersonality. TW felt right at home immediately as he was processed with barely a word beyond the technically necessary and ushered to a room facing north on the eleventh floor. He glanced at the view, unzipped his suitcase, shed his coat and went back to bed.

Rejection Hurts

In Café Franck Agnestina abandoned her Internet research into Maupassant and admitted to herself with a sigh that it was time she closed the computer, opened the book beside it and started to read the writer's own words, not those of the critics, commentators and academic busybodies who littered the web. She leant back against the banquette, curled one foot under the other knee and began to read. She was soon engrossed in a story, all thoughts banished of historical context, the place of the author's style in the development of French literature and whether the sympathy for female characters denoted early feminism.

A commotion at the door made her look up, and a gaggle of three boys and a girl swept through the curtain, talking loudly and happily. They grabbed a table by the window and began to shed their coats and bags. The girl was elegant, with a full figure and shoulder-length brown hair, wearing a high-necked cashmere jumper that guaranteed she would be noticed. One of the boys she had never seen before, though another she thought might be an occasional member of her class. The fourth, the one laughing loudest and moving to the bar to order, was Flamand.

Clearly he had not noticed her. It felt strange that he was with new friends, but then she hadn't met him since before Christmas, so she supposed it was inevitable. Then Flamand turned in her direction, surveyed the room indifferently and turned back to give his order to Patrice with a smile. He had seen her, she was sure of that − no straight man since she was fourteen had failed to notice her glories, her blonde hair − but not a glimmer had registered. It was as if she was part of the wall itself. Agnestina was not used to being furniture. Should she go and say something, ask how his holiday had been, how his family were? Flamand carried a tray of coffee and beer to the table, sat down with his back to her and quite deliberately put his hand on the brunette's knee.

Agnestina lowered her head in shock, opened her book and tried to focus her eyes on the words. They refused. Instead they began to gleam with tears. She told herself it was absurd. She had been embarrassed by Flamand's lovelorn poetry all through the autumn, had let him sit at her table, nothing more, rather as a dog was permitted to lie under it, and then had staged a little scene just to show who was boss. She had treated him like a dog, but that was the way it had always been with boys throughout her teenage years − the way it should be.

Shouldn't it?

After a few minutes she quelled the tears and steeled herself to look up. Flamand's hand was no longer caressing her successor's knee (he was in animated conversation with the boys). The scene was worse. The girl was caressing his.

Perhaps for the first time in her life Agnestina felt lonely – not just the boredom of being alone, but the numbness of actively being unwanted. It hit her like a brick in the stomach.

Gathering up her computer, coat and book she left her seat, walked by Flamand's group without a glance and went round to the other end of the bar counter. Patrice was waiting for her.

'I know. I saw,' he said, before she had a chance to decide how to begin. For a moment she gazed at the floor.

'Can I have a drink?'

'Of course,' said Patrice, and looked at the bottles behind him, wondering what would be best for her melancholy. Then the professional barman's manner deserted him. 'But you know, it will not help. Go home, Agnestina, have a long bath if you can, pack for Italy. Remember, tomorrow you will be in the mountains – a different world.'

She nodded, tried and failed to smile, and left Café Franck without another word.

Had she not she would have caught Flamand's glare of fury as the curtain closed behind her. The point had been made, but there was no pleasure in victory.

Catrina would have been pleased with the scene, however, except for Patrice's sympathetic words. She was having to admit that her usual insecurity was beginning to cloud her responses. Certainly Agnestina had an unfairly high place in her thoughts as she waited for her MEP, Gwyneth, to come back from lunch. The office was quiet and snow continued to float past the window high up in the Parliament building. The backlog of emails from Christmas and New Year had been dealt with or junked, and the normal stream of invitations, reminders and complaints was not up to speed. Nothing much was coming out of Wales either, since it was even more impenetrably snow-bound than Brussels, and few people had made it into work. Catrina clutched her mug of coffee and stared at the snow, absently wondering whether it was coming down at home in Derbyshire too.

Ever since Nikita had insisted Agnestina join their jaunt to Bolzano, Catrina had been in a silent dither. She had agreed to go because she had been asked, more than anything, and it meant a first weekend away from Brussels with Patrice – time when, though with friends, they would not have to worry about the shifts at the bar and when they could concentrate on themselves in surroundings that were neither of their usual territories. He had agreed, she supposed, for the same reason – or maybe just because the whole thing was a free adventure. Patrice had shown no obvious interest in Agnestina, but he had been the one to introduce her into the equation. It might have been an accident that she was sitting at a convenient table with a computer when they had wanted help – but she was not the only she. She was just the one Patrice had spotted – and he had spotted her because she looked gorgeous.

When Gwyneth Price came through the door Catrina hid all the churning going on inside and asked whether it would be OK if she took off Thursday and Friday – she knew she had only just come back from holiday but something had come up and it would be a big help if it would be no problem and (she paused for breath)…

Gwyneth smiled. 'Not a problem. To tell you the truth I'm skiving as well. My young man is flying me to Corfu till Monday. It won't be hot, but it can't be worse than Brussels and Machynlleth.'

That was the end of it – no discussions or searching questions, for which Catrina was duly grateful.

The Joy of Work

Some time in the middle of Wednesday afternoon Mercedes realised that Fidel would be baffled not to find her at their hotel when he was returned from visiting Elise by her brother. It was surprising, she frowned, that he had not been in touch. Mercedes was lying on her bed in the new expensive hotel, the oldest in Bolzano, having a holiday snooze while the short day waned, rain gradually giving way to snow, and Rory was downstairs going about his journalistic business. Her wet socks had been exchanged for woolly slippers, her wet jeans for the sumptuous hotel bath robe.

She rolled over, picked up her phone from the bedside table and sent Fidel a text telling him that they had moved. Then she lay flat and closed her eyes, feeling her duty had been done.

Within seconds the phone buzzed and, eyes still closed, she answered with a grunt.

'Mercedes?' asked the unsure Fidel.

'*Sí.*'

'I wondered.'

'I'm sorry. I should have told you earlier.'

'Oh, no – that is nothing. I went to lunch with Artur, you know – Elise's brother. A delightful young man.'

'Good.' She could have sounded more delighted, but she was sleepy, thinking more how pleasant it was to be warm and lying in luxury rather than trying to look busy at her desk in Nikita's gallery.

Fidel took no notice. He was not the sort to catch or be worried by a nuance once he was talking. 'Interesting too. I wish he was one of my students.'

'I thought you had resigned,' Mercedes observed, not meaning to cause trouble.

'Resigned? Certainly not. I was forced out by dark forces, people with no understanding of my subject, students who had no talent, a university determined to throw away all my experience, despite all I did for them.'

'Oh,' said Mercedes, not interested enough to argue and sensibly failing to add, 'So you did resign.' Instead she moved the conversation on. 'We are at the Hotel Laurin. It is where Nikita wants to stay. Do you want to move too?'

It was Fidel's turn to grunt. 'What's it like?'

'Very comfortable, expensive – traditional, you know, like in films.'

For anybody else the answer, given that he was not paying, would have been a simple yes, but for Fidel yes was never simple. How would it look if he, a man of socialism, a man never seen even with combed hair on television, were to be seen in the company of Europe's moneyed wasters in a five-star film-stars' hotel?

The answer could not be otherwise. 'No, I will stay where I am. I do not want to have to pack up again, and my view of the mountains is quite satisfactory.'

Mercedes smiled. The mountains had barely been visible at all since they had arrived. 'If that is what you want. I don't know if there's a room here anyway, but I could have checked. Perhaps you would like to come over and meet us this evening?'

She clicked off the phone and pulled the duvet over herself.

Some time later she half awoke to realise it was dark and that Rory was in bed beside her.

'Don't wake up,' he whispered – and then touched her in a way that gave her no option.

She giggled. 'If you say so.'

After a while, when Rory had turned on a bedside light, and they were lying on their backs looking contentedly at the ceiling, he asked, 'Do you think we are degenerate enough to ring room service and demand tea, cakes and half a bottle of champagne while we dress for dinner?'

'Half a bottle?'

'Slip of the tongue. A bottle.'

'And all on a workday.'

'Even worse.'

'I think the hotel will have seen behaviour like this before in the last hundred years.'

'Maybe you're right – we'll just continue the tradition, shall we?'

Mercedes rolled over and stroked Rory's chaotic hair. 'Do you think Amelie and Esko will do this when they arrive?'

'If they have any sense – and she is a film star. I think we should do the research for their scene. Don't you?'

There was time for Rory to shower and dress before the waiter knocked on the door. He did, it was true, feel as near as he ever had to being in a scene from an early Bond film, with his dark-haired Spanish beauty demurely hidden under the bedclothes while he found a tip for the waiter, watched as the trolley was placed by the window and let the champagne be opened by an expert.

'So was your afternoon useful?' Mercedes asked after Rory had shown the waiter out and she had sat up naked to receive her glass.

Rory thought this was first time he had ever briefed someone in such a distracting state on the doings of a European commissioner. 'Very – if you mean, did I get a story.'

'Do you want to tell me?'

He collected his own glass and a plate of small cakes, and came over to sit on the bed. 'To us,' he said, raising his glass in toast. 'Well, eventually Mr Venetian Republic reappeared, and he did not look happy. He basically stormed out, stamped around outside in the cold while his car was fetched and his minions tried to be nice to the manager.'

'You think his meeting was a waste of time?'

'I think Commissioner Redetti gave him an almighty bollocking in forceful Venetian dialect.'

'You think or know?'

'As it happens I know.'

'Did she tell you herself?' Mercedes was prepared to be impressed.

'Not quite,' confessed Rory. 'Once Borelli had scooted off I hung around and went to the bar, and sure enough, a couple of Redetti's assistants came in. They ordered beers and I asked for a gin and tonic, very loudly and in English, which meant they felt safe enough standing next to me speaking Italian.'

'Is that important? I mean, can you understand?'

'Just because I am Scottish and don't speak Spanish does not mean that I have an ear made of tin.' Rory chided her. 'I spent my Erasmus year in Bologna, so yes, I do speak Italian – quite well enough to follow a conversation.'

'I'm sorry.'

He brushed her apology aside and filled their glasses. 'What they said, apart from how Borelli would probably be ballistic for quite a long time, was that Redetti is staying here for the weekend too. I thought it would be the other way round. But I think this is about to become a working holiday.'

'Have you sent the story?'

'Not yet.'

'Now?'

Rory looked at his glass, looked at Mercedes and said, 'Not just now.'

Mercedes reflected, as she sipped more champagne, that if this was work, she could cope.

VI

Thursday

That Frozen Feeling

Queuing in the snow on Thursday morning at not much after eight-thirty for the increasingly complicated and temperamental electronic gates of the European Parliament was the least glamorous part of an assistant's life, and one that Bruno resented. He had been in the job for only a year and a half, but even in that time the security systems had been revamped at least three times and shifted between three different entrances. As far as anyone could tell the only benefit had been to the guards, who now regarded themselves as supreme beings. Bruno did not feel safer, he just felt very cold, and wished he had stayed in bed. He reflected that if somebody wanted to kill him – somebody other than Catrina and Mariana, that was – now all they had to do was take a Kalashnikov to the queue or chuck a grenade at the glass towers so that everybody was done in by falling sheets of glass. As it was, hypothermia was likely to get him before any terrorist.

In front of him was a tall blonde head that he thought he recognised. He stared at it for a while – a distraction from wondering if the tops of his ears would snap off. They all moved forward four paces and stopped again. Bruno looked down at the rest of the woman's figure in case it gave him more of a clue as to whether he had just seen her passing and liked the view, or whether he might actually have met her. The bulky red anorak told him nothing, and he was too close to be able to peer below it without causing comment. Another shuffle took them to the bottom of the parliamentary steps. Progress.

On the fifth step the woman removed one glove and reached into the pocket of her anorak, drawing out her pass. The lanyard caught on the pocket's zip and the pass dropped to the icy stone. The woman swore and bent to pick it up, butting Bruno, one step below, in the stomach, which made her miss the pass itself. She did not apologise, but started the manoeuvre again.

'Here, let me,' suggested Bruno, and stepped aside from the strict line to reach down at a less acute angle.

The woman turned, retrieved her pass with a nod but no word of thanks, and began to turn back, then stopped. 'Oh, it's you.'

Bruno could not deny it, but was no further forward than the original vague feeling of recognition. 'It is,' he admitted. 'Forgive me, but I…'

She moved up two steps and Bruno made it three, bringing him alongside and giving him the uncomfortable insight that he was the shorter by some distance.

'We met, or nearly met, yesterday when you came to talk to that American lobbyist from Ziggie Industries.'

'Ah, that's it. So we did.'

That seemed to cover it really. Bruno remembered TW had looked fairly shaken by his encounter with her, and that she had been brusque to the point of surly with him. She was bloody tall. Dutch, clearly.

They shuffled forward, not speaking again until they had passed through the barriers and stripped off their coats for the fun of the metal detectors. As they rose up the escalators, the woman, by now a step below (and so on the same eye level) tapped him on the back.

'Did your member meet him?' she asked.

'Yes, they had lunch on Tuesday. Quite a long one.'

They reached the level of the third-floor concourse and Bruno had to get used to being looked down on again.

'Oh dear.'

'Why?' he asked.

They moved a pace away from the escalator so as not to cause a blockage.

'I need a coffee,' said the Dutchwoman. 'Shall we both have one? Then I can tell you.'

'All right, if you think it's important.' Bruno tried to sound nonchalant, but he was curious.

She shook the melting snow from her hair. 'Important? For me no, but it could be for you.'

They crossed the concourse and the bridge to the Parliament chamber and the Mickey Mouse bar beyond, bought coffee and croissants (separately, going Dutch) and found a couple of chairs by the window.

149

'I suppose, the thing is,' Bruno began, trying to sound diffident and charming, 'I don't really know who you are.'

'Saskia van Katwijk. I know who you are.'

'I suppose that's nice. Do you want to tell me how?'

'Not really,' announced Saskia and moved on. 'The reason I am talking to you is because I think you ought to know that letting that man Wangstrutt talk to your member was a bad move.'

'Why? He seemed harmless enough to me.'

'Harmless, possibly, but Ziggie Industries are not necessarily so. That is not the problem either, though. We have found that neither Ziggie nor Mr Wangstrutt have bothered to put themselves on the Transparency Register as lobbying, so it is a big breach of Parliament rules. I'm glad we checked. You should have done too.'

Bruno looked sheepishly into his coffee. This woman had a point. 'Bugger!' he muttered.

'Possibly,' said Saskia without smiling. 'Also, his name is not popular in the Netherlands. His family were complicit in the annexation of us into France by Napoleon in 1810. It is possibly why he is now an American.'

That was, thought Bruno, hardly something he could hold against TW personally. Saskia was right, though. The rest was a mess.

'Any ideas about what I should do?' he asked.

Saskia shrugged and rose. 'None.'

As she strode away Bruno watched her confident, disdainful back and decided she was the most frightening woman he had ever met – at least, among those under the age of fifty.

Saskia banished him from her mind entirely. She had given him information. She had done enough – especially for a pathetic Englishman.

Wrong Milan

Nikita's idea of packing for the weekend was to find a suitcase only just within the limits allowed by airlines and to empty her wardrobe into it, swearing spectacularly in Russian (a very good language for swearing in) at the impossibility of remaining civilised with so few clothes and, with extra venom, the utter depravity of airline officials who imposed restrictions that would have prevented her forebears from leaving their dacha for so much as lunch!

After tipping the clothes on to the floor, she marched through to the kitchen, made the making of coffee sound like the crashing of a lorry's gears and resisted the temptation to lace her demitasse with a breakfast brandy. No drink till the airport, she admonished herself.

Calmed rather than energised by the coffee, she returned to the task with more method. Shoes and make-up, the two categories from which it was most difficult to select because one just never knew, were also unfortunately the heaviest. Nikita wondered whether it was conceivable to travel with only one pair of boots, one set of sensible indoor shoes and a selection of three for the evening. And who but an urchin could arrive in a fashionable ski resort with only a single bag of foundation, eyeliner, lipsticks, moisturisers, powders and eyelashes? At least in Italy there were shops which understood what enhancement a woman needed.

Underwear was always a problem. Probably nobody would ever see it, but if the mood came upon Nikita she could not be caught out wearing dreary cotton or an ill-matching bra. As for the exhibited clothes, she must resist the urge to wear all black, or all white, and there was the heat of the hotel and the cold of the mountains to consider, and the need to look *sportif* as well as *chic*. Hopeless!

Despite everything Nikita made the 14.35 flight to Milano Linate without it having to be delayed and even with a case that was two kilos within the regulations. There was a little fuss about the size of her handbag, but only a little – and she was through security in time to have a swift sojourn of caviar, smoked salmon and half a bottle of champagne before she began the dismal trek to the distant gate.

There were many things that Nikita did not include in her self-image, and one of them was 'economy passenger'. She would like to be first class at all times, but since such a distinction was no longer possible on European flights, she was prepared to sink one step to business. She was a businesswoman, of course, though she felt that as long as the gallery paid its rent and enabled her to keep her domestic standards up, it was really a higher calling, a service to humanity: art for those who used their brains as well as their eyes.

She settled into seat 3A and wished fervently that no one would squeeze into 3B. She liked to spread. The capacious handbag had contained another, more modest, one in beautifully tooled Moroccan leather that held her most essential fortifiers, and she had no intention of sticking it under the seat in front of her unless absolutely necessary.

Nikita was in luck. Not only was 3B uninhabited as the doors were closed and the inane cartoon of safety information switched on, 3C was empty too. This should have been a perfect arrangement, she thought, as she accepted the warm flannel and glass of water proffered while they taxied out to the runway, but it did mean that the rather delectable Italian man in the superbly cut grey suit was sitting with his back to her in unreachable 2C. She wondered whether, a little later, it would be acceptable to stumble against him as she found her way back to her seat from the minuscule toilet.

After take-off boredom began to set in as they climbed, but the captain stubbornly declined to switch off the seat belt sign. The tedium was relieved when the middle-aged stewardess, wearing even more foundation than Nikita herself, arrived with a consoling flute of champagne and reassured her that it would not be the last, though also reminding her that this was a short flight and they would be over the Alps and into their descent within the hour. Nikita slugged back a gulp of wine, held out the glass for more, making it clear that therefore good drinking time was not to be wasted. She was disappointed and just a touch chastened to see that the good-looking gentleman in front of her had taken only fizzy water and was examining graphs on his computer. Her interest evaporated even faster than the bubbles in her indifferent champagne.

On landing the handsome specimen made for the exit carrying just his briefcase while Nikita waited, forlorn and a little tipsy, for her twenty-one kilo trunk to emerge on to the carousel. First the belt carried luggage from the Barcelona and Athens flights before, and just as the Brussels passengers were about to revolt, the screen announced that their bags were in the hall.

For Nikita the message was premature. She did not know it but, as she stood with a look of sour irritation at the cases starting to move into view, her belongings were just landing across the city at Milano Malpensa.

She waited. After a while her co-passengers all drifted off with their belongings, and she had the first glimmerings of apprehension. She glanced at her watch. Nearly five. Eventually, when the screen announced that the baggage from Berlin was about to arrive on the belt and Germans began to jostle Nikita for the best spot to grab their bags, she wandered over to the airline desk and presented her boarding pass with its stuck-on luggage tag. The handling rep scanned the bar code, frowned, scanned it again, tapped on his computer, shrugged, scrolled up and down and finally raised his eyes to confront her.

'Signora,' he began, the apology already encompassed in the tone, 'so unfortunate, so regrettable.'

'What is?' Nikita glared as only a slighted Russian can.

'Your baggage is in Milano, but unfortunately not in this Milano. It rests in Malpensa – so sorry.'

'And?'

The shrug grew. 'Signora may wait here. We hope, but nothing is certain, that the bag will be brought here within three hours—'

Nikita shrieked, making the poor man jump and drop his mouse.

'Or,' he continued, 'if the signora will tell me where she is staying it can be brought to her before midnight anywhere in Milano or Bergamo.'

'But I am staying in Bolzano,' Nikita growled, her voice dropping almost two octaves from the shriek. It was a dangerous sign.

The shrug was gargantuan. 'In such circumstances, signora, the suitcase will indeed be delivered, but not until tomorrow – maybe morning, possibly—'

He was to complain to his wife later that evening that he had never been called such appalling names by a passenger, a woman, or in so many languages.

Once Nikita had given the hapless serf the address of her hotel she stormed through the arrivals hall, where a driver was waiting patiently with her name on a board. He made the mistake of asking if she had any more luggage, and turned a little white at the reply.

Still standing on the curb by the Mercedes she dialled the human Mercedes, who had been expecting a call but just assumed the flight had been delayed. After a curt explanation, Nikita had only a baleful wail left.

'What am I going to wear?'

Still Life

By Thursday afternoon Elise was bored – a very good sign. Her headache had all but disappeared. Legs and ribs hurt abominably if she moved too much, but if she did not her pain sensors switched off. There was no need to spear herself with morphine every few minutes – just a dab if she did something daft, like try to turn over too quickly. If she lay still, or only used her arms when she was propped up against the pillows, she could almost believe she was returning to normal. Only when she used the hateful bedpan, or was subjected to the nurse's brisk bed bath, did she feel the extent of her troubles.

By contrast to the afternoon the morning had been busy, at least for a while. After the rituals of nursing and the doctor's round (all smiles, satisfaction and nods of encouragement, which Elise only half trusted), her brother Artur had arrived with cakes and sympathy. Once he saw she was well, though, he had made his excuses and, telling her that the rain of the day before had disappeared, had headed for the ski slopes. His sister's predicament had done nothing to put him off.

Fidel had arrived, propped up by Mercedes, twenty minutes later. He was little help, though, and the struggle of moving about on his injured ankle meant that it was he, not Elise, that seemed to be in greater need of nursing. Fidel apologised, did his best not to look pathetic, tried his hardest at some political banter as Mercedes recounted the story of Rory's near-encounters with the European Commissioner and the Venetian separatist, then admitted that he was not quite his normal self, and would spend the rest of the day resting. He allowed Mercedes to escort him away as soon as an hour of visiting time had drifted by. She threw a backward smile at Elise, as if to say, 'Don't worry, everything's under control.' She had also warned her of the arrivals overnight – of Nikita, Catrina and Patrice – and the possible appearance on Friday of Esko and Amelie.

Elise groaned. 'I feel like a fool – and like Exhibit A.'

The expectation of multiple visits all through the next two days did nothing to dispel the boredom of Thursday afternoon. It was time for everyone else's siesta, which meant that even the nurses settled into an hour or two of disinterested relaxation. Elise was too ill to feel like reading or dealing with the messages and news on her

Exhibit A

phone, and it was low on battery anyway. She must remember to tell her brother to bring her charger next time. All the radio stations available through the earphones attached to her bed were in German or Italian. But doing nothing made her think – and thinking made her bones hurt again.

For the first time since she had come round from her concussion and sedation she thought about what she might have been doing had her snowboard missed the rock. The strange thing is, she would have been doing nothing remarkable – perhaps sitting on the chairlift with her brother as it carried them up the mountain for another run, grateful to be on the slopes again after the wasted day of rain. They might be a little glad of the mountain air to clear thick heads after a night of hot spiced wine.

She thought too of the difference between her old body and the one that she inhabited in the hospital – how lithe and fast she had been, how careless of physical strain or difficulty, how oblivious to, or judgemental of, the limitations of others. Always before last Sunday agility had come naturally to her. She could not remember a time when her body did not respond as she demanded. Now it languished and hurt, held together by the skill of doctors and the efficiency of chemicals and machinery.

It was odd, too, how her fall had changed the plans and experiences of so many other people. It even, if Mercedes was not embroidering her account, might have changed the reporting of and the course of politics. If she had missed that rock, Fidel would be sitting in Flagey with his beer or plotting revenge on his university. Esko might be weekending with Amelie, but not in Bolzano. Rory would be getting to know Mercedes a little better, but not as well as he did now.

Nikita would be finding something to do in Brussels – she had no idea what, but it would not have involved paying out a fortune for a vanload of acquaintances to come and play with her in the Dolomites. A European commissioner would not be dealing with the premature discovery of a meeting with Venice's new champion.

After a while the warmth of the room, the quiet and the remains of the drugs in her system had the effect they were meant to, and Elise drifted from boredom into sleep, letting her broken body concentrate on the slow business of repair. The sleep was shallow, though, and it was hard for her to know which were thoughts and which just dreams. She thought about being in bed in Brussels, and then her dreams wondered why she could not get up; she knew she was late for work in Café Franck. Fidel would be at his table waiting for her to start so he could follow his routine of not ordering a second beer until her shift began. Damien would be complaining that he had to collect the cups and glasses himself. Patrice would be making jokes about her if he noticed at all.

In fact, Patrice had already left the café, and was on his way to the airport with Catrina. They had booked an early evening flight so they could finish most of the day's work. Patrice had joined up with Catrina on the platform of Central Station for the airport express with, for her, amazing ease. They had brought the minimum of luggage, but that meant that Catrina spent most of the ride wondering what vital item she had forgotten. Only when they were safely in the air did it hit her – make-up! Patrice would have relished the joke that his lover and his hostess, Nikita, were in precisely the same position.

A German Adventure

The only member of the party after Monday who decided to take the land route from Brussels to Bolzano was Agnestina – after all, she had recommended it to Mercedes and Fidel, even if it meant getting up horribly early. She had some good reasons for taking her own advice, she told herself. First and foremost was the fact that, although she had been on planes many times in her twenty years, she had never taken a train down the Rhine and through the Alps. Then there was the chance it gave, between glances out of the window, to get ahead with some of the stack of books that she had promised her tutor she would read over Christmas and had failed to dismally. Just to prove her intention was serious she had lugged seven with her – admittedly mostly slim volumes, but to show she meant business she included the selected works of Racine and a truly grim collection of critical essays on existentialism.

There was an element of guilt in her third reason. She was very aware that she was travelling on Nikita's money and generosity – her student budget would only normally allow for coffees on the journey, and she was carrying her own supply of fruit and self-assembled baguettes, her one indulgence being a pair of fresh warm croissants bought at Gare du Midi almost as soon as they came out of the oven. She was also aware that she really had no excuse for joining the trip.

She did not know Elise, had no ties to any of the others and only the most tentative connection to any of them thanks to Patrice (who was nice but a bit old). The guilt, though, came from her inability to imagine travelling with Nikita.

The feeling was nothing definite, just an indefinable sense in her gut that taking to the air with her Russian host would be excruciatingly embarrassing. There was the hair (stacked and sprayed), the coat (real fur – how could she?), the loud Russian voice and gestures, the politics and tastes of the woman twice her age. The last four excuses would have been unfair. Nikita was not as old as she sometimes dressed, she could be perfectly restrained and demure in public when she wanted to be, and her politics were irreproachably gentle. There was no escaping the fur coat, however.

As it turned out, Agnestina was wise, given Nikita's tantrum over lost baggage by the evening. Much earlier, while Nikita was in the final throes of packing, Agnestina was changing trains in Frankfurt, swapping her early morning express for the sensible and more leisurely one that would carry her across the Austrian border to Innsbruck. She had selected her seats on each leg of the journey carefully, making sure she would be nearest the river on the train and facing the engine so that the mountains would gradually greet her in the distance from Frankfurt onwards. The reading had gone well – she had finished a Flaubert novella before Cologne and annotated several Rimbaud poems before Mainz; somehow perfect words as she wound along the west bank of the Rhine, even if she was enough of a literature student to know that the German romantics should have accompanied her.

Agnestina settled herself into the window of a four seat group with a table in between and laid out her next three books and a large flask of coffee (cheaper than at the station). At first she was alone, but just as the whistle blew and the doors rolled shut, a woman slipped into the seat opposite. Without looking up Agnestina corralled her belongings into a neater collection on the table and selected the dreaded existentialist commentary. There were many miles of average Germany to travel through before the exciting mountains.

The first hour slipped by, the turgidity of the critical prose made little more riveting by frequent sips from the flask and half the brie-and-tomato baguette. Then a particularly incomprehensible and inconclusive paragraph destroyed what was left of her patience and Agnestina sighed, closed the book and let her eyes rise to the landscape of northern Bavaria as they sped towards Nuremberg.

The eyes of the woman across the table were closed and Agnestina studied her with the same dispassionate curiosity she had given to the countryside. The woman was good-looking, Agnestina decided, admiring the thick flourish of nut-brown hair, the sculptured cut of the jaw offset by high cheek bones that suggested a touch of Slav. She was perhaps five or six years older, the French girl thought, and her clothes – pale-yellow jumper with a high neck, elegant woollen trousers to match her hair offset by a forest-green velvet jacket – were expensive and gave the hint of a professional already doing well, or maybe just plenty of money in the background; not married, though – or at least not wearing a ring to signal it.

Agnestina should have blushed as the woman's eyes opened and caught her in the act of assessment, but there was something about the instant half smile and the knowing but welcoming eyes that made a blush unnecessary.

'Hallo!' The greeting was in English.

Agnestina smiled back.

'I'm sorry, my French is not good enough to use to a Frenchwoman.' There was a nod towards the books.

'And I have only a little German,' Agnestina replied.

'Then let us continue in English, since otherwise we cannot know each other. I am Heinke.'

'Agnestina.'

'We are so of our countries, I think. I shall be stopping in Munich – will you be too?'

'No, to Innsbruck and then to Bolzano.'

'Oh, you are skiing?'

It was the obvious question, but one for which Agnestina was wholly unprepared. She had thought about being in the mountains, about seeing a new part of Italy and about sitting around with the Brussels crew, but taking to the slopes herself had not occurred to her – absurd, she realised. She could ski; in fact, she had spent two weeks of the previous winter doing just that above Grenoble, and rather well.

'I will be there only for the weekend, but I hope so.'

'A weekend is enough if the snow is good.' Heinke looked a little puzzled, wondering why this beautiful French girl would be travelling all the way to an inaccessible corner of Italy if it was not to ski. It would not be for work, clearly, given the student's pile of books and notes. The only other possibility was a lover or family. She would know soon enough. 'Are you going home this way too?'

'Yes, on Monday – that is the plan.'

Heinke drew a business card out of her jacket pocket. 'Then perhaps you might like to see Munich, unless you know it already.'

'No, I do not.' Agnestina picked up the card. It read 'Heinke, Gräfin von Starnberg'. There was no job title. She decided not to think too hard. 'Perhaps I would.'

By the time they arrived in Munich, and after a little lunchtime wine provided by the Gräfin to go with their conversation, it seemed an excellent answer.

Intelligence Gathering

If Lucia Redetti, the European Union's Commissioner for Regional Affairs, had hoped that her meeting in the rain-soaked depression of a Bolzano hotel on a wet Wednesday in January had gone unnoticed, then she was disappointed. It was true that there had not been any TV crews hanging around when she had arrived to talk to Sanzo Borelli, the firebrand Venetian separatist, but they were outside the doors of the hotel on Thursday morning. Only because the rain had stopped, one of her staff had observed, with the cynicism that always governed the relationship between the political system and broadcasters: a relationship symbiotic but mutually destructive.

Redetti resigned herself to not worrying about how they had found out, assuming that some local journalist had recognised her and rushed to tell as many newsrooms in Milan as he could. She was surprised, though, when her press secretary called from Brussels and told her that that was where the story had originated – with a ten-paragraph item filed overnight on the English-language website of *Europe Now*, the paper that the Commission thought of as its only friend. The office knew that was the origin because nothing had hit the print editions of the Italian papers and the online editions had carried no more than the Brussels version, spiced with lots of suitably lurid speculation. This was being added to steadily by non-specific claims ranging from great things to insulted outrage from 'friends' of Borelli, who was never happier than when there was plenty of huff and no puff across the news wires.

Luckily the hotel manager, furious that his venerable establishment was being doorstepped by scruffy cameramen, had forbidden them entry and had erected strategically placed event screens across the lobby so that guests, especially Commissioner Redetti, would not be spied on or spooked. That way she had at least managed to walk through reception for a private early-morning dip in the hotel pool before the inquest on the previous day's meeting started promptly at nine – in the office in Brussels they would have met at least an hour earlier, but this Dolomite trip was meant to be a mixture of work and pleasure.

The staff of three who had accompanied her were faced with a Signora Redetti who, while not being in one of her moods, was not the relaxed and cheery boss they had been hoping for either.

She read through the print-out of the article, removed her glasses and asked quietly, 'Any idea how they got this?'

All three looked sheepish, but there were no volunteers.

'Not, I mean, the fact that I was here on the same day as Borelli – any fool from the drinks waiter to the driver could have told them that. But they would have told the Italian media, not Brussels, and it would have appeared yesterday, while Borelli was still around – not late last night, and not in such knowledgeable detail.'

The answer to Redetti's interrogation was simple enough. Rory had planted himself on a bar stool and ordered a gin and tonic, relishing the Southern disregard for measuring spirits in puritanical thimbles as was the practice in Britain, thanks to Scottish King James VI's distrust of publicans to serve legal portions.

The tall tumbler that faced him, even allowing for the small iceberg, was filled to receive little more than a mild dilution of tonic. He sipped it happily, letting the kick of the gin and the sourness of the juniper invade senses that had been brought to fever pitch anyway over the previous hour.

Taste buds indulged, he looked along the bar at his fellow drinkers. There were three loners at the far end, each with the depressed air of boredom common to men who are faced with a lonely evening in a hotel populated by couples enjoying themselves or work parties booked in together. There were two stools spare, one next to Rory and another on the other side of the only woman at the bar – in her early fifties, Rory reckoned, and sitting so that it was clear she had nothing to say to those around her. After a few minutes she finished a Campari and soda, ordered another and made her way through to the dining room.

A rare couple, German by the sound of them, came and occupied two of the stools, leaving only that next to Rory free as he studied the wall clock, trying to decide if he should have more gin before Mercedes appeared. Worth risking.

Midway through his order the stool next to him was filled by a bloke his own age, dressed like a man on business who has just ditched the tie for the evening. Rory recognised him as one of the entourage who had arrived with Redetti and had spilt the beans about the reasons for the visit when talking to his colleagues earlier. Not noticing Rory he demanded a whisky on ice.

'As I was saying,' Rory continued, 'yes please, I would very much like another gin.'

'Oh, excuse me,' his new neighbour said, 'I did not realise…'

'No problem. I'm sure your need is greater than mine,' grinned Rory. It was as good an opening as any.

'You are Scottish?' The Italian accent was heavy.

'I am – and if I was you I'd choose another whisky than that, even if you are going to kill it with ice.'

'But you are drinking gin!'

'Because I'm mixing – wine earlier and later. If I do that with whisky I'll be no use to anyone tomorrow.'

And so it was that when Mercedes arrived looking spectacularly Latin and exotic, Rory thought, a while later he had the whole story of Redetti's stay in Bolzano and it had cost his employers precisely three whiskies, two of them rather good malts. For his companion the cost came in the morning when he admitted at the meeting that he might just have said more than he should to the nice Scotsman he had met at the bar and who had said he was just in town to be with his new Spanish girlfriend while she took care of her boss, arriving the next day. All of which was true. Somehow the little matter of Rory being a journalist had never arisen.

Against Expectations

The are moments in every life where one just has to give in and stop fighting. For Tyron Wangstrutt Thursday morning was one such. His immune system had resigned, his temperature had left him semi-delirious and his legs could barely carry him across the room. He was in the grip of full-blown winter flu, and there was nothing much to be done about it until the virus had had its way with him. He lay in his expensive room halfway up the garish modern monolith of the Hotel Dutoit and ignored the tweeting, the beeping and the insistent ringing of his phone. In truth he was hardly conscious of them, such was his fever.

When the chambermaid, a no-nonsense Romanian in her late thirties, gave up waiting for a response to her knocking and used the pass key, she took one look at the prone TW, crossed herself, covered her mouth and left to tell her housekeeper and announce that she was not entering the room again until she had been given a mask and the doctor had been summoned. She needed the money too much to catch flu herself. She also knew how serious flu could be. In bad winters in Brasov, in Romania's poverty-stricken years, she had seen it carry off two uncles. They had looked all too like TW did that morning.

So it was that he missed ever more desperate early demands from Washington to 'clarify' his position vis-à-vis the

European Parliament's Transparency Register, his dealings with MEPs and just how he intended to get Ziggie Industries out of an even bigger mess than the regulatory soup they had sent him over to sort out. Saskia, it seems, had wasted no time in reporting Ziggie to the parliamentary authorities, they to the Commission and the Commission, through lawyers almost as expensive as Ziggie's own, to the company's Chief Executive. Since the regulatory soup involved a minor sum of around three billion dollars it was probably just as well that TW was mostly unconscious.

Over in Esko's corridor of Parliament that Thursday morning there was nothing as dramatic on the cards. His assistant, Mariana, had a strand of the Baltic Lutheran in her character that made turning up for work late very hard to do – so hard that the guilt it induced effectively wiped out the pleasure of the extra stolen hour in bed. So it was that, even though she had left the voting sheets on Esko's desk the night before and had no need to see him before he left for Nice, she was nonetheless at her place in the office at the hour demanded by her contract.

Still, Esko had beaten her to it, and though his overnight bag showed he was in the building, he had already collected his papers and headed out into the body of Parliament. Mariana reflected that, since he had become a Group Leader, she saw an awful lot less of him – or perhaps they were just avoiding each other in the aftermath of her emotional turmoil; turmoil not quite banished. She spent a lonely but efficient morning, working on her report into freedom of expression – trying to make it her own, rather than just a rewrite of the briefing from Dirk van Abcoude, the Secretary-General of European Writers

Against Injustice (EWAI). She answered the torrent of emails coming in from all sides, including a chunk from Finland that tried to get Esko to commit on domestic issues about which she knew he would remain neutral (and so answered as blandly as she could).

She expected to see him at lunchtime, as soon as the votes were taken, even for a few minutes when he came to collect his bag on the way to the airport, but the minutes crept by and he did not reappear. Mariana stayed at her desk until half-past one, then gave up and dropped down to the canteen. By the time she returned at two, the bag was gone and so, therefore, was Esko. A kind but hardly necessary note on her computer keyboard apologised for missing her, hoped she'd have a good weekend and promised to spend as much time with her as she needed on Monday.

Mariana grunted, screwed up the paper and hurled it at Esko's door.

The ball of paper was in mid-air when the other door opened and the urbane figure of Roberto Vincenzi, Esko's disgraced predecessor as leader, walked in. He watched the missile land, but made no move to pick it up.

'My apologies, Mariana – am I interrupting?'

There was no short answer she could give so the question was ignored. 'I thought you were in Rome.'

'I was, and now I am not,' Roberto replied reasonably. 'Where is Esko? I have some information for him.'

'On his way to the airport.'

'Ah – home to Finland?'

'No, to Nice.'

Roberto raised an eyebrow. 'In January? How eccentric. It is almost as cold as Helsinki. No matter. I must go to the airport myself – Milano in my case. Maybe I will meet him at the gate, maybe I will just telephone him tomorrow.' He left.

Those few minutes were crucial. On such a little matter of timing great consequences turned. Roberto had been about to tell Esko that, although he was leaving neither the European Parliament nor the Group, he was becoming an independent member, though only for a week. After that he would be the first and only member of his own new movement – Italia per Tutti! was his first inspiration for a title, though not necessarily his last. The exclamation mark would be obligatory. This new arrangement would allow him to bypass the machinations around his old party, on behalf of which he was accused of losing some €600,000 in unexplained expenses. A new start, a new party and, he hoped, new accomplishments would flow. By chance, he had been offered an advisory position with an American company, Ziggie Industries, which would make the financing of his move less onerous – but now Esko would have to wait to hear the details.

The new leader of a party of one landed in Milan Linate in the early evening and made his way to the arrivals hall. In front of him a woman in a fur coat walked uncertainly. Roberto had a strange feeling he knew her, but then, he congratulated himself, in his position one met so many people.

Rescue

While Nikita was on the phone to Mercedes (who was listening with trepidation to her boss's tale of lost luggage), she was tapped on the arm.

'Hi,' said Catrina, grinning. 'I thought you were getting the earlier plane. We didn't see you on ours.'

'Later!' Nikita snapped at Mercedes and ended her call abruptly. She turned on Catrina and Patrice as if they had personally sent her suitcase to the wrong airport. 'I did take the earlier plane, and I have been standing inside waiting for my baggage ever since. It has, apparently, been sent to Milano Malpensa, and cannot be delivered until some time – any time – tomorrow.'

'Oh, sorry!' Catrina followed her policy of 'If in doubt, apologise'. Patrice looked at the chauffeur, wondering who he was waiting for, and they shared a glance which suggested that the rest of the evening would be painful. 'How are you getting to Bolzano?' asked Catrina. 'Can we get a lift to the station with you?'

'The station?' Nikita's eyebrows rose in a combination of astonishment and disgust. 'Why would I go to the station?'

'We have to get the train from somewhere,' observed Catrina reasonably.

'That would take for ever. And I don't take trains, except,' she conceded, 'sometimes the Eurostar or the Thalys. They remind me too much of Moscow. This car is mine.'

Only for the weekend, thought the chauffeur with relief.

'But that is excellent,' Patrice contributed. 'It is so kind of you to think of everything.' He began to move around to the far door.

As Patrice left her side, Catrina was aware of another figure at her shoulder. She half turned. 'Oh!' she said in surprise as she recognised Roberto Vincenzi.

'Forgive me, signorina, I think I have seen you in Parliament – perhaps with my good friend Esko Nystrom.'

'Yes,' admitted Catrina. 'I work for Gwyneth Price.'

'A formidable lady indeed. But I think I overheard *this* lady saying she had lost her luggage. Perhaps I can help?'

Catrina made the introduction before Roberto turned all his attention to Nikita.

'Sadly, signora, even I do not have influence enough to capture your suitcase before the morning, but this is Milano and the hour is not yet twenty, so I know a discreet emporium which will be pleased to furnish your needs until the airline fulfils its duty. May I accompany you?'

Nikita's whole demeanour softened. She melted into a smile that managed to be charming, playful and infinitely vulnerable at the same time.

Catrina looked from the Russian to the Italian and her puritanical Derbyshire heart rebelled. It was all a little revolting. Nonetheless she said nothing, and soon Roberto was between her and Nikita in the back seats while Patrice rode in the front with the chauffeur and they headed into the centre of Milan. They were passengers but, she realised as they pulled up outside an elegant shop window, carved out of a fine Renaissance palazzo a street away from Teatro alla Scala, for Roberto and Nikita they were something much more important: they were audience.

Roberto had pre-announced their arrival, and they were met at the door by the famous Leonora Grassi in person – black-haired and fuller of figure, but otherwise, thought Catrina, disconcertingly like Nikita herself when she ushered her instantly favourite potential buyers into her own gallery. Indeed this was the original Galleria Grassi: just with clothes instead of paintings.

Catrina and Patrice stood to one side, as if taking their seats in a box at the opera house round the corner, and watched as the performance unfolded. A click of the Grassi fingers summoned two assistants, one male, one female, to establish a balance of obsequious attention. The spectators and the two actors – Nikita leading, Roberto supporting – were handed flutes of Prosecco. The boy lifted off Nikita's fur coat, as though it was the dust sheet from a piece of exquisite antique furniture, and the girl, with a little murmur of apology at not being able to divine Nikita's exact measurements merely by eye, began to flourish her tape – not so much an article of science as an essential prop for her role.

Meanwhile, La Grassi talked of the glory of black if it was not allowed to be oppressive, how superb Nikita's figure was (a sentiment with which Roberto and, for that matter, Patrice agreed – and it was then that Patrice realised that Nikita was considerably younger than he had always assumed) and how a touch of pink could enliven winter in the Dolomites when ice was everywhere.

Half an hour later Nikita was equipped with two complete outfits – daytime trousers and cocktail dress, cashmere jumper, stockings, underwear of great delicacy though eye-watering price and a change of shoes – all courtesy, after token resistance, of Roberto.

Catrina, as though she had won the competition for best applauder in the claque, was granted a little burgundy jacket of such perfect fit that she felt as though she had been instantly transformed from a frump to a starlet – just as well if Amelie and Agnestina were going to turn up in the next few hours.

In the fitting room, out of sight of the older women and the men, her fellow assistant had made her strip to the waist, wielded the tape measure, and prescribed a new bra of completely different proportions to the one that Catrina had always assumed to be right ever since she had been sorted out in the Derby branch of Debenhams for her school graduation ball. Only once the new (and also free, she was told to her relief) construction was in place did she realise how off the mark the old dimensions had been. Nothing pinched or drooped any more. When she emerged in the jacket she saw from Patrice's smile that her new look had not gone wholly unnoticed.

Dinner followed the purchases, only a few metres away at a small ristorante of breathtaking refinement, at which they were joined by Leonora Grassi herself and her equally sophisticated husband – an art dealer like Nikita, it turned out, though only of sculpture, from Donatello to Canova. They talked about the reason for the trip, a story sufficiently long and complicated to see them through the antipasti and the pasta, and Roberto wondered whether indeed he might run into them all again before the return to Brussels.

There was no mention of politics, except a remark from Roberto that it was time for a different and more civilised discourse in Italian life. By the time they all slid back into the

Mercedes for the few hours' drive into the mountains, the three foreigners were besotted with Milan and happily tired. Their only duties had been to make sure Roberto would be an honoured guest at Nikita's next *vernissage*, his card safely stowed by Catrina but more private particulars noted on Nikita's phone.

An Actress Unimpressed

Had Nikita taken a few minutes more to finish her caviar and champagne in the departure area of Zaventem airport she would have seen Esko scurrying along to gate twelve to embark for Nice. He was a little late after the completion of the week's votes and the inevitable approaches afterwards to which, as party leader, he had to listen with patience, whatever his schedule.

That Thursday afternoon his schedule was simple enough: get himself to Nice, hire a car that would not make him look like a travelling salesman and take the road east towards Monte Carlo in time to pick up Amelie just after dark from her filming location in the mountains just above Monaco. They would spend a night in the most expensive square mile on earth before setting out across northern Italy on Friday morning.

Esko, the sensible forty-something politician from Finland, had a vision of himself as Marcello Mastroianni speeding round the Alpine hairpins in a nifty Alfa Romeo on his way to collect the delectable first lady of French film. The dream shattered as he climbed into the ever-sensible moderate Renault the car-hire firm had made available.

Feeling nondescript again, he edged his way out of the airport and into the stop-start traffic on Nice's coast road in rush hour.

Drizzle puckered the windscreen and to his right the Mediterranean ended the day as dirty grey. Esko was almost as frustrated as Nikita waiting for her luggage as he drove at snail's pace along the Corniche, looking for the exit that would divert him on to the right road (according to his virtual map) towards the trucks and caravans of the film unit high on the inland cliffs. He imagined Amelie sitting disconsolate in her caravan, removing the make-up and the costume of an eighteenth-century servant girl, tight bodice and all, who had spent the day peering out to sea for a sign of her lover's pirate ship. Who would be more upset by the late or non-arrival, he wondered, the actress or the servant girl?

Reality can be a cruel dampener of the imagination. Amelie was at that moment sipping a warming herb tea, with a chaser of cognac, in a cosy village bistro and listening with a rapt smile to Eugene, her director. The smile was rapt not because Eugene was fascinating, but because he had just asked if she would like to star in his next project, to be filmed the following autumn and set in Barcelona during the Spanish Civil War. The least she could do was to listen sweetly, and, to be fair, Eugene had only been mildly put out when she had told him (her fingers gently entwining with his) that she was leaving that night for Monte Carlo and a weekend in the arms of Esko.

Eugene had consoled himself with the fact that there was still a month of filming with Amelie to go. He was just calling for more cognac when Amelie's phone trilled.

'*Oui?*'

'Amelie, hi.' Esko had never learnt in Helsinki how to begin a call with endearments. 'Where are you exactly? I think I am about ten minutes away if you are where you suggested.'

'Oh, *cherie*, I am so sorry! You have passed us. You must turn back.'

'You've left?'

'Yes, we are in the village, the café Le Canard Soif. You can find it?'

'I can try,' agreed Esko and rang off.

It was unreasonable to be cross with Amelie. After all, she did not have to wait in a company caravan on a damp winter evening. It was natural to head off with the crew for a drink after the light went. Nonetheless, it meant adjusting his expectations, and that was always enough to make Esko cross.

When he arrived at Le Canard Soif the crossness was all too obvious. He shook Eugene's hand with the minimum of ceremony, refused a drink and made it clear that Amelie should finish hers as quickly as she could get it down. She glared at him, swigged, then rose from her chair, giving a Eugene first a long kiss, then a shrug full of unimpressed meaning as she collected her coat and bag. She as good as flounced out of the door while Esko held it open – a pointless gesture, since she had no idea which of the cars outside she was supposed to make for.

Esko was a silent Finn, but he had never before encountered a silent French actress in a strop.

By the time they were approaching the Monaco border and the lights of Monte Carlo he could bear it no longer. 'Sorry.'

Silence.

'Very sorry. That was ungracious of me.'

Silence – well not quite: there was a sniff. A hand flurried dismissively.

They passed the border sign.

'What shall I do – take you back?' he asked.

The other hand flurried.

'But do see the hotel first. It looks out over the harbour and all those Russian yachts. You may even find a racing driver in the bar. They're resting in January.'

Amelie snorted, but Esko suspected it was more laughter than disdain. There might be hope. He tried something very un-Nordic.

'And I do love you.'

Mlle Poitiers was too good an actress to react instantly. The silence continued, if with a touch less tension. As they inched through the streets winding down towards the sea, she pulled a packet of Gitanes from her handbag, selected a cigarette with care, lit it with the car's lighter, opened the window a fraction, inhaled and blew the smoke slowly out into the night.

'Do you?' There was no interest in her voice.

The non-smoking Esko knew he was being played, but she was forgetting he was Finnish, not Norwegian – he came from close enough to Russia for smoking to be normal still. And, since he had mentioned racing drivers, he put on his best Kimi Räikkönen growl.

'Often,' he said, pulling the car into the underground garage of his chosen hotel.

As he unloaded the two small suitcases, so much more economically packed than Nikita's, Amelie sat tight, enjoying the cigarette, now illegal inside the garage. Even when Esko came around and opened her door she was in no hurry, and she took a last drag and stubbed out the glow in the Renault's ashtray. Esko wondered if he'd be charged extra for cleaning when he returned the car at the end of the weekend.

In silence Amelie moved to the lift, letting Esko carry the bags. She stood back and smiled dispassionately as Esko completed the check-in formalities. Only when he had a collected the room key and a porter had collected the cases did she speak.

'Now,' she said, 'show me this view, then I shall decide.'

VII

Friday

Making Progress

Fidel was much refreshed by Friday morning. He had slept for nearly ten hours, and that after resting and dozing through much of the day before. Only the waitress bringing room service in the middle of the evening had visited him. He had had a hard week: the shock of the news of Elise, the turbulent dash south and his own disastrous fall. Switching out the lights for half a day had done the trick, it seemed. His lethargy had gone, and so had enough of the pain in his ankle to make the coming weekend less daunting – at least physically; the social side of it, with half Brussels ascending to the mountains, retained its perturbations.

The weather was better, too. For the first time since Elise had been on the slopes the sun had come out, the clouds reduced to occasional decoration of the peaks, and the ice had thawed on the city's pavements. Best of all Fidel's technique with the crutches had improved to the point where Mercedes and Rory no longer had to prop him up on the way to the hospital. He was not exactly swinging along, but neither was he looking like a drunk sloth and, after delivering him to Elise's bedside, they felt confident enough in his capabilities to leave him.

Elise herself was also recovering fast. All the tubes and drips had been removed, which automatically made her feel more normal. She had been encouraged out of bed and, while stiff and hurting in a dozen places, was able to stagger on the nurse's arm to the bathroom for a welcome shower. Back in bed, clean and with the pain subsiding, she looked so different from the broken waif of only five days earlier that Fidel and Mercedes were quite astonished. She had even felt well enough to send a text to her brother telling him to enjoy the ski slopes for the day and only visit her in the evening. Fidel arranged himself at her bedside, set his crutches down and smiled at her with his first genuine pleasure since they had said goodbye to each other in Brussels more than a very long week before.

Leaving their charges in the best spirits of the week, Mercedes and Rory returned to the hotel for their next batch of responsibilities. At least Catrina and Patrice had arrived to share the strain. The four of them had breakfasted together and caught up on the events of the week, finishing with Catrina's awestruck description of the superb dinner of the night before.

Neither Agnestina nor Nikita had appeared for the buffet in the dining room – Agnestina because she would rather sleep than dress for breakfast; Nikita because, after the trials of her journey (only partly assuaged by her rescue at the hands of Roberto Vincenzi), there had been no question about the necessity of breakfast in bed. She had little intention of presenting herself in public before midday.

The story left Rory a little jealous – not as a man, or even a gourmet, but as journalist. Once his story had been spotted and the leak detected, Commissioner Redetti and her staff had vacated the hotel smartly on Thursday morning, firmly though politely refusing Rory's request for a formal interview 'in clarification', instead thrusting a half-page statement into his hands, which was less than useless since it said almost nothing worth quoting and had also been released to the rest of the world too. The best he had been able to do for his editor was a rehash of the previous day's facts, a more extensive burst of speculation and a description of Bolzano that became more lurid as he tried to make it lively. Had he supped with Roberto Vincenzi he would have had a follow-up scoop that would have been as tasty as the meal. As it was, the best he could hope for was that Esko would feel like giving him a feature for the weekend edition, instead of just skiing with Amelie, though that would be worth a photo or two.

Like all good holidaymakers Rory had ignored the TV and online news sites first thing, only bothering to look once he had returned from the hospital with Mercedes and settled into the café across the road from their hotel – the same table from which his recognition of Redetti had sparked his interest.

'Good grief!' Mercedes heard him exclaim as she sipped the froth from her cappuccino.

'Something wrong?'

'No – it's a surprise, though. I may have to get busy this afternoon.' He showed her the headline. 'Redetti to lead Government?'

New Year had been turbulent for the weak Prime Minister of Italy and it looked as though his party was now desperately hunting around for a safer pair of hands and one, more importantly, that was not sullied by lingering scandal.

Mercedes was beginning to feel that having a journalist as a boyfriend was tiresome – he was too often distracted from the important details of life, like her and coffee.

'Oh, really?' She tried but failed to sound interested.

'So that meeting with Borelli may have been really significant.'

'Why?' Mercedes transferred her attention to a delicious almond biscuit that sat alongside her cup.

Rory looked at her, wondering for the first time whether he had overestimated his friend's qualities.

'Because I thought Lucia Redetti was meeting him here to explain, as Commissioner for Regional Affairs, that his attempt to lead Venice out of Italy was going to get nowhere. Now it looks like the opposite – she was probably coming up with devolution promises if he supported her in coalition in Rome. They couldn't meet in Venice – too much like Redetti swimming the lagoon for him – and he was not going to talk to her in Rome, so Bolzano was perfect.'

'Yes, I suppose it was. Lucky you were here.' Mercedes did her best to sound as if she meant it.

'Amazing really.' Rory's thoughts too were miles away. 'But why was he in such a bad mood when he left, then? I'd better make a couple of calls.'

He had been sensible enough at the hotel bar on Wednesday night to get a business card off Redetti's assistant, and now was the moment to pull it out of the wallet. Mercedes was about to see Rory the professional for the first time.

Autostrada

When Esko drew back the curtains in the morning, the view across the yachts of the mega-rich of Monaco was almost as good as it had been the night before when Amelie had acknowledged that the lights on the water were sufficient to restore her humour. She had pouted a little, required a lot of kissing and made the most of the hotel's champagne list, but she had eventually let Esko know he was forgiven. The sun was shining too weakly to make the day warm enough to breakfast on their balcony, but half opening the full-length window gave them the illusion without the chill.

The drive from Monte Carlo to Bolzano takes most of a day, especially if time is taken to get off the autostrada and find a half-decent lunch in Piedmont. Even if he started early Esko doubted he and Amelie would arrive before dark, and Esko had no intention of leaving early. He had never been to Monaco before, and he wanted at least to wander round the harbour and up to the Grimaldi's palace before he set off.

By ten o'clock they were repacked and ready for their stroll. Esko paid their bill with only mild horror at the price, asked the concierge to look after their bags, and they stepped out into the sunshine. To his astonishment there was a flurry of clicks as a score of photographers jostled forward. For a moment he had forgotten that Amelie was no ordinary partner – she was a French film star, and on a slow news day in January a film star in Monte Carlo was too good a chance to miss, even in that city of celebrities – maybe precisely because she was not seen there every day.

Amelie smiled sweetly, took Esko's arm to emphasise their togetherness and gently wheeled him round and back into the relative safety of the lobby.

'No sightseeing, then,' observed Esko.

'Not alone, I think.'

'Another time, perhaps. Let's go, then – see if we are less conspicuous in Italy.'

They retrieved their bags from the concierge who, mortified (though it was he who, for the usual financial consideration, had alerted the press), insisted that his deputy carry them down to the garage. The reason was not wholly altruistic. There was another potential bonus if he reported the number of the car to the paparazzi in case they wanted to give chase. Amelie was wise to that game, though Esko was outraged when she explained later, and stated firmly that no help was required. The porter was dismissed at the lift door.

'Until Italy I will drive,' Amelie announced. Esko looked quizzical but said nothing and handed over the keys.

The paparazzi had the sense to realise their quarry might be heading for the garage and crowded the pavement at its entrance. They were expecting a fancy sports car or at least a luxury four-by-four, and they were also expecting Esko to be driving – so when the innocuous Renault runabout appeared and swept away up the street, they not only nearly missed it, but they were also on the wrong side for the favoured shot of Amelie. The swearing was not pretty. One dogged cameraman ran to his motorbike, but was much too slow to spot the nimble Amelie turn right towards Italy instead of left for the Riviera.

As they shot towards the border Esko grinned. 'Filming a car chase yesterday, were you?'

'Next week. This is practice.'

'You can forget the stunt double, then.'

'All except for the actual crash.'

'Naturally. That would be expensive.'

Amelie giggled. 'In cars or me?'

'Both.'

As they headed for Genoa, Amelie showed that she was happiest at high speed. Even Esko, coming from a nation of rally and racing drivers, had to make an effort to seem impassive as she wove expertly between more moderate drivers.

An hour or so into the drive Esko's mobile rang. He looked at the screen and frowned. 'Roberto, hi. A surprise – especially because I'm in your country.'

'I know,' said Vincenzi, and explained that he had seen Catrina the night before by chance in Milan. 'I wondered if you will be passing this way?'

'Well…' A look at the map showed that they had a choice to make only a few minutes later: whether to head to the mountains via Milan or ride across the Po valley almost until Verona before turning north again to the Tyrol. 'Why? Surely we can talk on the phone? Or can it wait until I see you in the office again next week?'

'I think you will not thank me if I do either.'

Esko looked at Amelie for a signal. 'We really do not want to come into Milan. Traffic on a Friday.'

'Yes, that is understandable. You know Esko, I would not ask if it was not important. You almost pass through Brescia, whatever way you choose. Could we meet there at three? I will not delay you or Mlle Poitiers for more than an hour.'

'Brescia's traffic will be almost as bad. I will consult her. Hang on.' He did his best to sound doubtful. The last thing he wanted to do was switch out of his relaxed reverie with Amelie back into low politics. She grinned and decided to be of help.

'I've never seen Brescia, have you?'

'No,' admitted Esko. 'OK, Roberto, we'll be there. Text me with where to meet. Make it somewhere obvious and easy to park – and to get on the road again afterwards. You can buy us a late lunch.' He rang off before Roberto could protest.

'Do you mind?'

Amelie shrugged. 'Not at all, if the lunch is good and he is interesting'.

'That is about all I can promise about Roberto. He eats and talks well.'

'But I cannot manage another hundred and fifty kilometres without coffee if lunch is going to be that near sunset.'

'Coffee at Piacenza?'

'And you drive after that.' Amelie was arranging it nicely so that she could enjoy Roberto's wine. She saw Esko's face darken. 'I will let you concentrate on the serious things you have to discuss and make it up to you later.'

'How can I object?' he sighed.

Elegant Rising

Nikita arose from her bed rather as the Sleeping Beauty arose from hers – slowly, rather hazy about where she was and wondering if she could get some breakfast – but without the presence of a Handsome Prince. This was an omission and Nikita felt it keenly. Without one, the bed was losing its attractions, comfortable as it was. She reached for the room-service menu, dialled and placed her order: plenty of coffee, scrambled eggs with smoked salmon and the usual bread rolls, but with extra honey. She toyed with caviar, but even for Nikita the price was numbing. There was no hurry, she insisted – in fact, half an hour would be advisable to allow her to prepare.

Preparation when she was not in a hurry was a ritual for Nikita with as many little ceremonies and elements of significance as that devised by the high priest of pharaonic Egypt. There had been enough time at the airport the night before to restock with make-up essentials at the duty-free shop. Before a long and detailed shower there was the ceremony of the Laying Out the Bowls of Unguent: an introit. Then an army of tweezers, clippers and tongs was placed on a table close to a mirror of forensic clarity. This was for the torture session, the ritual cleansing that followed the more general hose-down.

In the pause after this section of the service, when Nikita was appropriately robed in white and towels enveloped her hair, the breakfast arrived, the trolley escorted by a waiter who only a maiden of the most ghoulish tastes could describe as handsome. Once it was clear that Nikita was unlikely to have banknotes in her hotel dressing gown, he departed with barely a glance, leaving her with a turned-down mouth, sullen with the thought of what might have been. She sighed, poured coffee from the silver pot, stabbed the salmon and commenced the process of rebuilding her face.

The first foundation layer had been applied when the phone by the bed rang. Nikita decided to be local. '*Pronto.*'

'Oh, I'm sorry,' a young female voice said in heavily accented English, 'I understood this was Nikita's room.'

'It is. Who are you?'

'I am Agnestina.'

'Who?'

'From Brussels.'

'Oh, of course you are. My dear, how stupid of me. You are here?'

'Yes, I arrived last night, but I could not find you.'

Nikita twiddled her eye pencil. 'Yes, we were late. At first it was a disaster, but then a sweet man came to my rescue.' Roberto would have been delighted by her description. Agnestina just thought Nikita was telling stories. 'And you?'

'Oh, nothing really. I was tired.'

'And what have you planned for the day?' Nikita was barely listening as she drew lines.

'I am going skiing. I was going to wait, but then when I did not hear from you I called the ski centre and they said I could rent my skis from them, so I said yes. Do you ski?'

'My dear, I am Russian. Of course I ski.'

'Oh. Yes, I see.'

'But not today – I have none of my clothes. All sent to the wrong airport by that stupid airline. I will have only what I bought last night until the luggage arrives.'

Agnestina sympathised. 'Did you pack all your mountain clothes?'

'Everything!' But then Nikita ran through the list of what she had actually put in her suitcase, and realised she had done nothing of the sort. She had packed for comfortable days in the hotel, a little stroll around town, and evenings in imaginary but delicious company. For the slopes she had barely a woolly jumper. How stupid! And she knew she looked good in those leggings.

Her tone changed. 'Are you going now?' She glanced at the bedside clock which read ten past eleven.

'Well, yes,' admitted Agnestina.

'And I suppose you will not come back before dark?'

'It is such a short day.'

Nikita thought quickly. 'Perhaps I could join you for the afternoon. Could you leave me all the details of where you will be and the name of the ski centre at reception? Maybe you could pause for lunch at one of the restaurants on the mountain and I could meet you there?'

'OK. I can do that.' Agnestina rang off before Nikita made it any more complicated.

Two hours later Nikita was sitting on a sunlit terrace sipping a Bellini when Agnestina swept her skis to a halt in front of her and waved. To those watching along the terrace it looked as if two stars from an Italian film of the 1960s had just stepped into the frame. Nikita had shopped fast and wisely. Her red anorak was open to a red jumper over the tightest of black ski pants and her eyes were shielded by large but not forbidding shades. When Agnestina pulled off her goggles, they and the mint-green stripes on her ski pants and boots were almost the only flashes of colour that distinguished her from the snow field behind her. Nikita would have been depressed, though, that at least two of the admiring men drinking around her assumed that they were mother and daughter.

'Hi,' grinned Agnestina, after she had unclipped and stowed her skis and reappeared beside the table. 'Have you been on the piste yet? The snow is perfect.'

'Not just yet. I thought after lunch. But I have rented and waxed skis. Are the runs difficult?'

'Not very – at least, not just here. There are more challenges at the top if you want them.'

'Maybe tomorrow.' They ordered a lunch that left no bulges.

'Hallo!' came a voice.

They looked up to find Patrice smiling down at them appreciatively. Beside him stood a tousled-haired man as young as Agnestina.

'Patrice, darling, good morning. Will you join us?' said Nikita.

'Good afternoon. Nikita, Agnestina – this is Artur, brother of Elise.'

'Wonderful!' exclaimed Nikita, and both women took their time to inspect the new arrival. Agnestina looked from Artur to Patrice and back again. Not bad, she concluded, but she just smiled gently. In his turn Artur caught her assessment and blushed.

In the background Catrina, dressed for the winter in Derbyshire rather than a Dolomite fashion show, blinked and felt very much the third woman in a foursome. She pulled up a chair at an adjacent table and dared Patrice not to join her.

The Great Secret

Catrina would have felt even dowdier had Amelie joined them all on the slopes on Friday afternoon as planned. She was spared that ordeal for her self-confidence, though, as the traffic out of Brescia left Amelie fuming in the passenger seat while Esko inched them forward. They were not the only ones heading to the mountains for the weekend, and the late lunch with Roberto had closed the small chink in the time gap between jams.

In truth Amelie had been fuming for long before that — in fact, ever since Roberto had ladled his charm over her, while making it abundantly clear that discussions about politics were boys' stuff, or at the very least way beyond the comprehension of a mere actress. Her role was to decorate and amuse, and Robert was fulsome in his appreciation, but unfortunately his reason for wanting to talk to Esko was weightier and the earth would shake. So once wine was on the table (for him and Amelie – Esko was predictably Finnish in only taking sparkling water before his driving stint) Roberto sank into a conspiratorial huddle of his own, whispering into Esko's armpit as Amelie at first just glared and then decided to drink as much white wine as she could sink, just to make him have to buy another bottle if the old goat wanted any.

Esko sat at an awkward angle, trying to bend enough to hear what secrets Roberto was aiming at him, while staying upright enough not to let Amelie think he was part of the misogynist conspiracy.

The Great Secret was, it turned out, about to be not a secret at all, and was equally likely not to be regarded by the rest of the world as enormously great, though Roberto believed it would be. He was informing Esko, his successor as leader of the European Parliament's Social, Liberal, Enterprise and Ecology (SLEE) group, that he wished to remain a member, even if the little fiscal matter of expenses accounting in Rome hung over him, and he was leaving his erstwhile local Italian party to start his own. Esko nodded. This was not news. What would have been news would have been if the little fiscal matter had disappeared over Christmas and left Esko's political annoyance tray by New Year.

'You,' Roberto tapped Esko's arm in comradely fashion while Amelie slugged back the wine, 'have been a true friend. I am sad to say that has not been as true of my fellow fighters in Italy. I have found almost no support from Partito Figli Garibaldi. They have left me to make my own way, so I shall. I am leaving them behind. From now on I stand for a new movement, a new conception, one that will offer a new way.'

'Oh good.' Esko tried to sound enthusiastic, but even he understood that new ways in Italian politics were as plentiful as olives. 'Do you have a name for the movement?'

'Of course. Grazie Italia!'

'Grazie,' agreed Amelie, as the waiter uncorked the second bottle she had ordered while Roberto announced his elevation from ex-leader in Brussels to founding leader in Rome.

Esko wondered whether he ought to ask for more details, ascertain whether political philosophy or just sheer fear and personal irritation was behind the formation, but one look at Amelie's increasingly dazed eyes decided him that this was not the moment.

'I thought first of calling it Italia per Tutti!,' Roberto confided — indeed, that was what he had told Mariana the name would be only the previous lunchtime, but political inspiration waxes and wanes fast. 'But I doubt if Italy will ever be for all, and I am not always sure I want it to be. I can call for thanks to Italy itself. That is honest.'

'Do you think Italy will be grateful?' Esko asked doubtfully.

'No, never,' admitted Roberto, 'but she cannot object.'

'You don't think that occasionally a TV comedian may suggest that the *grazie* stands for half a million euros?'

Roberto was pained. 'That would a misrepresentation of the truth, a calumny.'

'Naturally. Such things do happen.'

'It is my belief that I, as a political leader, should always thank the voters.'

'And hope that they say thank you back, Roberto?'

'That would be pleasant.'

Esko finished his water and refilled. He glanced across at Amelie who, bored and now warmly tipsy, was giving a delighted waiter the eye. 'I thank you too, Roberto, for letting me know before the rest of the world. Very helpful.' He made a move to stand, but Vincenzi had not quite finished.

'Of course, I still have my seat in the Senate.'

'Of course.'

'The old party is not part of the Government, and the Prime Minister only has a majority of one in that chamber.'

'I know.'

'But Grazie Italia! could be helpful, under certain conditions, which would double the majority.'

Esko grinned. He could see where this was going. 'The conditions being an end to allegations over expenses – and perhaps a ministerial position?'

'Oh, nothing so grand!' Roberto tried to look shocked. 'But perhaps the investigation could be widened to include similar loans to all other members, particularly in the lower house – and maybe there is a committee that needs an active president.'

'No doubt.'

Esko guided Amelie to the car, both of them feeling slightly sick – one from wine, the other from an excess of oil and duplicity. Nearly an hour later they finally edged past the last bottleneck in the autostrada traffic, and began to have a sense that the mountains were close. By then, though, the winter light was starting to weaken, and Amelie felt the stirrings of an afternoon hangover. Esko looked across at his sullen lover and reflected that the perfect getaway weekend was proving to be rather hard work.

When they eventually reached the hotel, darkness had filled the valley, though there was a faint glimmer of the sunset touching the high peaks. They were greeted with civility but without fuss (Amelie was, after all, a French film star, not an Italian or German one) and shown up to a room that, they were told with pride, would have a delightful view across the gardens in the morning. Amelie announced that she had a headache, would recover if she could, and would see Esko later. Dismissed, he changed into a thick woolly jumper and jeans and headed downstairs to the concierge. If he wanted a happy and peaceful start to the morning it would be sensible to have the star's ski gear reserved in advance.

Brushed Off

When Bruno was instructed by his MEP boss, Tony Sanderson, to track down TW and read him the Brussels equivalent of the Riot Act (a rather more gentle affair than its Westminster original), he thought it would be easy enough: just a swift visit to the hotel bar where they had warmed themselves the previous Sunday.

Nothing was ever quite that simple, of course. He was courteously informed that, *malheureusement*, 'Monsieur Wanstroot' no longer resided at this hotel. He had departed in some distress on Wednesday. However, if monsieur could wait, the information as to where Monsieur Wanstroot had moved to could be found – eventually.

A small consideration changed hands. The information appeared remarkably quickly. Bruno was soon walking back down Avenue Louise.

TW was in his room. Indeed, he had not left his room since he had first tumbled into it and the virus had struck – the virus that, to TW's fevered brain, seemed to have the combined force of bird flu and the bubonic plague. Nonetheless, by Friday afternoon he was not better, but felt that he might live. All was not right, though, as he knew not just from the incessant sneeze and the fuzziness of brain and breathing, but from the unaccustomed sensation that alcohol sounded revolting.

Even less appealing was the idea of checking his phone, reading urgent text messages from Washington and California or clicking through a forest of emails. The world was on hold. So when the bedside phone rang he seriously considered ignoring it too. The ring was loud, sibilant and reproachful. Unlike his cell, he thought, which he could turn down – or off – the bedside creature rang as it wished. Just to return to precious delirium he picked up.

'Wangstrutt.'

'Oh, hi. It's Bruno. Glad you're still in town.'

TW relaxed. Bruno he could handle. 'Good to hear you, son, but you find me on the rough side. Seems I got some kind of bull flu.'

'Sorry.'

'So am I. So if you are wanting to renew our friendship at the bar, it's going to have to wait.'

'Yah – well actually, TW, it was a work thing—'

'That'll have to wait too, son. I ain't seeing nobody, no how, no time.'

'Ah, oh.' Bruno was stuck.

TW surveyed the nerve signals from his substantial body and found them in better shape than he expected. He relented a fraction. 'You could try me tomorrow, boy, 'bout this time, and see if I'm on the mend.' He downed the phone.

'Right,' said Bruno to the dead line. Tony Sanderson would want things fixed by the time he hit Brussels again on the coming Monday. Bruno grinned helplessly at the receptionist as he replaced the house phone. He was at a bit of a loss. He could go home to St Gilles, only one stop on the metro, but it was Friday afternoon and the idea seemed dull. Now he was absolved from dealing with TW he wanted to play.

Out on the street the snow still lingered, but the sky was clear and a crust of ice kept the slush at bay. He had no plans and let his feet decide for him. He crossed the traffic and ambled past the fancy clothes shops at Stephanie, retracing his steps along Avenue Louise. Soon he found himself plodding downhill to Flagey. Must be some masochistic urge to relive the ghastliness of Sunday's encounter with Mariana and that appalling gallery, he thought, grimacing. The justification, if one was needed, was that there might be some weekend jazz, and the chance of a pick-up if he could be bothered.

Stepping through the draught curtain his spirits lifted (there was a jazz threesome giving it their best), then plummeted (there was Mariana at the nearest table glaring at him with Arctic intensity). Bruno nodded civilly and gave her no further attention as he strode to the other end of the bar.

'Beer?' asked Damien, recognising the Englishman.

'Why not. Give me a blanche.'

'Big?'

'Go for it.' Bruno suspected he might need it to frighten away the Glums. Looking around, tall glass in hand, there was no one he knew and few spare seats. There were three at Mariana's table, naturally. That was not an option worth considering. He searched the other end of the L-shaped room, close to the musicians. With perfect timing two suited men, incongruous in the twenty and thirtyish crowd, stood and prepared to leave. Bruno homed in on their table like a mosquito to a heel. A table to himself. Luck was on his side.

Next to him at the bar Flamand went through the same routine. He had no qualms about asking to share Mariana's table. He had never met her. His only disappointment was that Agnestina was nowhere in sight. He had come especially, just to see if time without him had softened her disinterest.

Mariana appraised the new arrival and decided he posed no threat. His French was too fast and imprecise to be a foreigner. She sipped her inadequate white wine and wondered whether he would try to talk to her. If it was going to be a French conversation, it was likely to be a short one. Despite nearly a year in Brussels, Mariana's command of the language was strictly functional. There was no immediate danger. Flamand drank his small glass of beer and pulled a book from his satchel. She noticed, though, that every time the door opened he looked up. In hope, or expectation? she wondered.

Plainly the next woman through the door was not for him. Flamand returned to reading his book as Saskia swept in. She recognised Mariana from Parliament, but they had never spoken, so they merely nodded their recognition of the connection and Saskia in turn went to order a drink. Once secured, there seemed few chances of a seat, just as there had been for Flamand. Saskia was not the standing sort, however, despite her length. She frowned and scanned the room again. One seat looked spare – a bit too near the band and facing away from it, but needs must. She pushed through the bar queue and sat down, then looked up.

'Oh, it's you!'

'So it is,' Bruno acknowledged. He wondered if his early evening had just taken a dive for the worse.

What Might Have Been

The doctor, a pleasant woman with grey hair that never stayed in place (and so made her look even more permanently harassed than she was) appeared at Elise's bedside soon after dark, just before the supper trolley was due. She smiled. This was not encouraging. In Elise's experience that week doctors only smiled when some part of your body was in even worse trouble than the pain suggested.

'I have some good news,' the doctor began.

Elise doubted it, but did her best to smile back.

The doctor seemed determined. 'You have made excellent progress – remarkable. You know there was a moment, quite a long moment, on Sunday night when we thought that the probability was that you would not survive – or that if you did, yours would not be an easy, perhaps not even a cogent life.'

This was a shock. Elise had hurt, had known there had been hours when awareness had gone and taken more hours to come back, but she had never understood that she had been in danger. 'Oh' was all she managed to say.

'Even the next day we could not be certain.'

'Oh.'

Was the doctor trying to scare her, or just impress on her that the hospital was clever enough to bring her back from near death? Either way, she could feel the nodules of pain (which had been almost forgotten in the afternoon sun) beginning to reassert themselves for the night.

'But now,' the angel of doom-laden cheer continued, 'I think we can be sure that it will be safe enough to allow you to leave us on Sunday – under certain conditions, of course.'

'Of course,' echoed Elise.

'We will check again in the morning, but for now, continue to rest.' The doctor's smile lapsed as she replaced the monitoring charts and moved on to the next patient.

Elise lay back in the silent room and stared at the spot on the ceiling that had become such a friend in the days of drips and morphine – it was only two days before, but it seemed an age ago. The parts that hurt now were at least countable; there was little of the general agony, just a dull all-over ache that told her she was mending but not yet mended. A touch of the ribs could induce a yelp, her bruised arm and thigh were sore, the wrenched knee throbbed a bit and the stiffness just below her buttocks told her that the pelvis had not enjoyed being landed on so hard. Otherwise, though, there was nothing urgent to report. Then she thought about rejoining the outside world, the January cold penetrating her bruises and bones, the slow trudge up the hill from Flagey to her flat carrying bags of shopping, stairs, standing for hours as she worked at the bar. Not yet, surely?

Suddenly she knew what it would be like when she was old – so long ahead, but real in a way it had never been before. Old age was what happened to other people, like being born a man.

She shivered and pulled the hospital blanket up to her neck.

That was how she was lying when the deputation of visitors, fresh from the ski slopes and fortified by a little après-ski, found her. Behind Nikita, leading like a captain, trooped Patrice and Catrina, Mercedes and Rory, Esko and Amelie and her brother Arturo on the arm of a blonde girl whom she vaguely recognised but couldn't place.

'Well, my dear – look at you!' exclaimed Nikita.

And they did. The chatter stopped and all nine stood around the bed and stared silently down at her. Elise went from fear of being old to fear of being laid out on the pathologist's slab or embalmed. She was a specimen of injury, Exhibit A in the Bolzano Municipal Museum of Alpine Accidents. She was being displayed as a warning to all reckless snowboarders – an education in every bandage. Perhaps she should throw the blanket to the floor, pull up her nightdress and let them all prod her bruises and inspect the contusions. Or maybe she was just a fish. Then she could just gape back from her aquarium.

'Hallo,' she tried.

She half expected them to leap backwards, yelping 'She speaks!' in astonishment.

Instead Catrina grasped her hand. 'God, you look awful! What did you hit?'

'A mountain.'

'Horrid mountain,' said Catrina, and for the first time in a week Elise giggled. It hurt like hell, but it didn't matter.

'You really came so far, all of you, to see me?'

'And the horrid mountain,' Catrina added with a grin.

Nikita took charge. 'Darling, we had to get your sweet old man out to you, so I sent Mercedes and Rory—'

'I know. It was so kind of you.'

'Nonsense, darling. Brussels in January is just too ghastly. We were all jealous of your holiday, though perhaps not this part.'

'And I wanted to see Amelie away from her film location,' Esko contributed.

Elise smiled up at Amelie. 'Another drama.'

'But I think this will have a happier ending,' said the star. 'Do you still feel bad?'

'Bad, yes, but at least I am feeling something, and it is not so terrible as anyone expected, they tell me.'

Esko had his serious face on – the one he used for delivering unhelpful economic statistics. It made Elise feel instantly better. 'The doctor has just told me I can leave the hospital on Sunday. They thought I would die, and I failed to.'

There was silence as the import of what Elise had just said sunk in. Even Nikita paused, conscious for the first time that her plan for a happy holiday jaunt could have had a very sombre outcome. She soon rallied.

'That's marvellous! We thought you would be in for weeks, didn't we?' She surveyed the rest of the group, expecting automatic agreement. 'Now we just have to get you home with us on Monday.'

There was a murmur of dissent from the other side of the bed. Arturo spoke up. 'We still have another week of our holiday here. It's all booked. I think we should stay.'

'Yes, we should,' Elise reached for his hand. Brussels and its problems could wait.

'Who are all these people?' a nurse barked from the doorway. 'We have limit of three visitors per bed. Now go, all of you.'

Chastened, the troop retreated, leaving Elise blissfully alone to enjoy the warmth of her bed and the ebbing of the pains the last hour had generated.

VIII

Saturday

Who Got Ticked Off?

To the few habitués of the Café Franck the place seemed deserted on Saturday morning, though to the general irregular populace the throng at the bar for coffee, croissants (and maybe a stronger restorative) seemed as impenetrable as ever. With so many of the usual clan clustered around a ski lift in Bolzano or enjoying the hospitality of the Italian hospital service there was little of the usual easy camaraderie or fraught suspicion to be fostered. Flamand sat stirring his black coffee unnecessarily and stared at the lake as Arthur might have stared waiting for the Lady to appear in her charmed boat.

Mariana was quite all right, thank you, wrapped in a black scarf so thick around her neck that it was quite hard to bend forward enough for the cup to meet her lips. She was equipped with a full morning's reading: *Le Monde*, *Der Spiegel*, two ecological journals from Finland and one socialist Belgian French paper just to show she belonged.

Damien, the smaller, younger version of Patrice (not as quick with his service, but much better when Patrice was not about), darted along the bar with authority, harassing strangers into early decisions. He missed Patrice and Elise badly – not because of their friendship, particularly – though he was cordial with Patrice and thought that one day he might feel like falling in platonic love with Elise – but because there were two less people suddenly to run the bar and clear the tables. Stand-ins had been found, but neither knew the ways of the café like the originals.

Fidel would have been furious had he known that his usual table had been occupied, perfectly deliberately, by four of his most despised university colleagues, down to whom news of his ill-fated romantic dash south had percolated. A toast to his painful ankle was raised in small beers.

A kilometre or so away, in the tower of the Hotel Dutoit by the Louise metro station, Bruno was pacing the foyer impatiently waiting for TW to emerge from the lift. The impatience and the pacing were both becoming more pronounced. Bruno had called the American from his pad in St Gilles at an hour when in theory only moguls had breakfast meetings. Such had been the instruction from his boss, Sanderson, that Wangstrutt was not to be given the chance to leave Brussels before a few (well, one) harsh messages had been delivered.

TW was an old hand, though – expert in knowing how to keep his hand the upper. Among his preferred ploys was to make sure he was early for his superiors (unless he could claim time differences as an excuse – he knew how hazy

Californians were about the vagaries of European zones), and late for juniors like Bruno. A week ago the boy had had his uses – now TW needed him to know his limitations. And that meant waiting; at ten fifteen the moment felt right.

The lift doors opened and for the umpteenth time Bruno paused in his stride and looked across. He was rewarded. Tyron Wangstrutt strolled out, dressed in a sober tweed jacket and lemon-yellow jumper over black trousers – a schoolmaster instead of the flamboyant business executive. He gripped Bruno's hand without a trace of a smile and led him to the comfortable armchairs that softened the brittleness of the modernist design. An attendant was summoned and TW courteously demanded a pot of coffee for two without consulting Bruno.

There were no preliminaries. 'That was a helluva bug you gave me,' TW announced, planting the blame firmly on the Englishman even though he had been germ-free for months – kept free of infection by frost and daily vitamins.

Bruno had the sense not to argue – at least, not with that first assault. 'Good to see you're better, Mr Wangstrutt.' He could lay on the chill of distance adequately too.

'Not better but functioning – enough to get whatever's eating you out of the way.'

'I'm not being eaten by anything,' Bruno countered, 'but you may soon be adding to your hyenas.' His encounters with Saskia had taken his difficult meeting technique to a new level.

'How's that, son?'

'Mr Sanderson has not been convinced that your approach—'

'Through you.'

'Through me, as you say, was above board. He has been alerted that neither you nor your company—'

'Corporation.'

'...had completed the required checks with the Parliamentary authorities for lobbying members or their staff.'

'Bruno, you're being pompous, and it don't sound too good.'

'I'm just telling you—'

'And I'm just telling you, young man, that Ziggie Industries, represented by yours truly, was very happy to stand your bar bill last Sunday night, with no thought of favour – just a courtesy to a man come out of the snow in distress.'

'Yes, well—'

'And further,' there was a pause while TW dispensed coffee to himself, unwrapped a biscuit and nibbled it thoughtfully, 'while I was having a conversation – not wholly satisfactory, I grant you – with Miss van Katwijk, I was delighted to accept the luncheon invitation extended by you on behalf of Mr Sanderson for that moment in a restaurant that, though convenient, could hardly be described as the sort of place Ziggie would normally regard as adequate if it was seeking to gain influence. Mr Sanderson seemed reluctant to pay even his share of the bill, so in the spirit of the same courtesy I showed to you, I avoided a scene with the restauranteur by picking up both our tabs.'

'But you discussed—'

'We discussed whatever Mr Sanderson wished to discuss. After the considerable amount of wine he ordered, I cannot quite recall what that might have been, especially since I was in some distress with the early stages of the infection you provided. Now, if you'll forgive me I have another engagement. Thank you for the coffee.'

TW rose, leaving Bruno wiser but poorer by fifteen euros. Defeat was expensive, he was finding.

Over at Café Franck, Flamand abandoned the book he had been trying to read and decided he had better places to be lonely on a Saturday morning, though he was not sure exactly where. On his way out into the bitter wind he was jostled without apology by the towering figure of Saskia on her way in. So Flamand joined the lengthening list of those who found her objectionable.

Skiing and Not

Saturday morning on the snow at the height of the Dolomite season is as much about exhibition as prowess downhill on strips of wood (or whatever variety of synthetic fibre is in fashion). Amelie, Nikita and Agnestina knew that they exhibited well and looked superb as they swished and sallied across the slopes – especially splendid when they reached the bottom of the piste, side-stepped to a halt and threw back their goggles. Artur was more than capable of holding his own and Esko, though less glamorous, had been virtually born on a pair of skis, and so his effortless technique drew admiration almost as great as that for those more lithe of body line.

Patrice was competent, but had not skied for several years. He would have needed a few lessons to reach a decent level, and one weekend was not time enough to bring back the skills. There seemed little point in pottering about the nursery slopes, so he was quite content to try a little desultory snowboarding, at which he was a true beginner and, in between attempts, to join the other non-participants in the sun on the viewing terraces.

Those non-participants were Mercedes, who announced that she was a child of sand, not snow, Catrina, who had no faith in her co-ordination and was genuinely terrified of going fast unprotected on anything, and Rory, who had tried skiing a few times in the Cairngorms and always found it a sure way of looking like a cold, wet idiot, and honestly preferred the pleasures of sitting in the sun with the two girls to showing off his unimpressive sporting attributes. He had a hope, too, that Esko would tire faster than the others and grant him an interview over the pre-lunch spumante.

In the hospital Elise, having told Fidel she would be fit to leave on the morrow, was back in her familiar role of trying to explain to him that the practicalities would not be as formidably difficult as he assumed. She, after all, could walk – though the process was still nothing like normal – and Fidel's sprained ankle was beginning to be less of a hindrance as he mastered his crutches. Their Brussels flats, one on top of the other, both upstairs and in a building halfway up a hill that was a challenge even in good weather, were going to be more difficult, granted, but as long as they were in the luxury of Bolzano's hotels, there would be little to worry about.

'But we have to go home on Monday,' complained Fidel.

SATURDAY

'No we don't. Artur and I have another week here. Has Nikita bought a ticket back for you yet?'

'I don't know,' Fidel admitted.

'Then you need to ask her. If not, she can get one for the same journey I am on – unless of course you do more damage to your leg and they put a hard cast on: then you'd have to go by train.'

'Why?' Fidel was perplexed.

'They won't let you on a flight in case your leg is a bomb.' Elise could sense a grumpy rant brewing, and quickly added, 'But you won't make it worse, will you?'

Fidel grunted and waived the impossible question aside. He had another problem to deal with. 'Will I stay with you? Your room will be too small.'

That was a fair point. Unlike the five-star palace that Nikita had insisted on, Artur and Elise were in a hotel that only just managed two stars, even in Italy's optimistic system. Her room was a single – very single.

Suddenly she was tired of the conversation and the decision-making. Surely the whole point of having a professor more than twice her age as a partner was that he was meant to solve tedious matters like this. 'We'll think of something,' she said with her eyes closed.

Fidel was not stupid enough to miss her expression. He took her hand. 'Yes, I will,' he said, changing the direction of the duty.

On the terrace above the end of the ski run Rory was just on to his second beer (and Mercedes and Catrina were on their second Bellini) when his phone burbled that a message had come in. He looked at the number: his editor. On a Saturday morning? Either the world was ending or he'd been fired.

Italian PM falls. You're there. Get on to it.

Rory's language found a word in vernacular Scots that Mercedes didn't understand but made Catrina snort into her cocktail.

'I mean, just because I'm in Italy doesn't mean I'm in Rome,' Rory thundered. 'In fact, we couldn't be further from Rome and still in this ruddy country if we tried. Why they think I'll know more about what's going on when I'm having a beer in a ski resort than they do in Brussels when the PM goes beats me. Editors are all the same – they get into that chair and forget how to read a map.'

'What's up?' asked Catrina.

Rory showed her the text.

She thought and sipped. 'There's always Esko.'

'Oh yeah, right. He's from Finland. Lot of help.'

'He's also a group leader, and he's here.' Catrina waved her glass at a figure speeding towards them down the final slope. 'He'll have more of the right numbers on his phone than you have.'

'Aye, you might be right at that,' admitted Rory. He stood up and started waving frantically at Esko as the Finn slithered to a halt. There was a nod of recognition.

Esko dismantled his skis and joined them. 'I hope that means you have a beer waiting.'

'Almost,' promised Catrina, catching the waiter's eye.

Rory said nothing, but just handed the phone over. Esko read as he pulled over another chair.

'Ah, yes. I was expecting this.'

'You were?' Rory was impressed and irritated at the same time. He always considered it a professional insult when the politicians turned out to know more than the journalists.

'I saw Roberto Vincenzi yesterday, in Brescia on the way here. He told me this might happen, though we thought it likely next week, not today.'

'Vincenzi – isn't he the one who—?'

'I expect so,' Esko cut him off.

An Interview

Leading a group at the European Parliament may not have originally been among Esko's ambitions, but he was still a polished and clever politician. He knew how to turn an unexpected situation to his, or at least his group's, advantage. When Rory told him of the Italian Prime Minister's resignation, and therefore of the probable fall of the government (yet again), he was ready with some news and an opinion, even after a hard morning's skiing.

Rory was equally able to switch into professional mode. 'Mind if I record this?' he asked. 'I left my notebook at home.'

'Not at all. If your phone is good enough you might even be able to use the audio.'

'Great,' said Rory, fiddling with the settings.

There was a pause while he tested the machine and Esko had a sip of his beer. Mercedes had lost interest, though she was pleased for Rory that he was getting an interview. Catrina was enough involved in the political world herself to pay attention.

'Right. Ready?' Rory asked. Esko nodded. 'Esko Nystrom, leader of the SLEE group at the European Parliament,' Rory paused to allow space for easy editing, 'were you surprised by the sudden news that Italy is to have a new leader?'

'One learns never to be surprised by such things in politics,' he answered, 'and in this case I was only surprised by the timing. Next Wednesday was a more likely date.'

'You mean you had prior notice? Nobody else seems to have done.'

'In a way, yes. Discussions with my colleague Roberto Vincenzi yesterday made clear that this was likely. He is intending to make his own announcement soon.'

'And what will that be?'

'You'll have to ask him. I'm not at liberty to disclose that since it is an internal Italian matter.'

'Can you give a hint?'

'No. Whatever he decides, he will have my support, as I made clear to him. But you must have had your own suspicions about the position. After all, you wrote about Mrs Redetti's meetings here earlier this week.'

'Nothing so imminent seemed likely.'

'It never does. As you know, my presence in Bolzano this weekend is a complete coincidence, but, it appears, a fortunate one.'

'Indeed. What is your assessment of this announcement?'

'Well, the coalition here has been unstable for some time, and I assume the PM decided it was never going to get any easier to manage or that, even if it was possible, he was not the man to do it. The crucial thing, though, is that Italy stays united.'

'You think there is a danger it might not?'

Esko paused, signalling that he was moving into serious and reflective mode. 'United Italy is relatively new, its current state not much older than my own country. There are older loyalties, long memories and affiliations. Most of all the divisions between north and south that are found in almost every nation are particularly stark and unresolved here. It takes considerable skill and powerful institutions to hold the regions together.'

'And you think that hold is slipping?'

'From the outside, it looks possible.'

'And what might that mean?' Rory pressed.

'I can't speak for Italy – I have no right – but I can speak for Europe. Italy is one of the original six member states of the European Union, and still one of the most important. The EU is at one of its periodic moments of difficulty, without the necessary degree of prosperity to ensure a decent living for all. At such moments we all need the senior member states to be stable and positive.'

'Can you say that will be the case?'

'At such times nothing is certain. The EU has neutralised the old animosities, but it has also made new entities and confederations imaginable. Who can say what people may want if they tire of old solutions.'

Esko made the cut across the throat gesture with his finger to show Rory that he'd said enough. He grinned silently and went back to his beer.

'Aye, I can work with that. I appreciate it,' said Rory.

Mercedes rejoined the conversation. 'Does that mean we will not have to leave for Rome immediately?'

'With luck,' said Rory.

'You may not need to at all – at least not today,' Esko promised. 'Once you've filed your interview with me I'll give you Roberto's number and one for a friend of mine in the PM's office who speaks good English.'

'Very good of you, but why not now?'

Esko smiled. 'Because I want my piece to have a chance.'

'That's news management!' Rory objected.

'Not that strong.'

Rory sighed. 'All right. I'll make do. I should go and write this up.'

Esko was on top of this too. 'Why don't you just text back your editor and say you've got the audio file, and he can have that now, but that you'll write up the context piece later? That way you and I get two bites.'

'You've done this before,' grinned Rory.

'You're right. I have.'

Catrina looked sorrowfully at her empty cocktail glass and then at Rory. 'I notice that your sudden popularity with the editor doesn't run to expenses.'

'No – but now that I've been on duty I think Parliament will be pleased with us.' Esko waved the waiter over for another round.

'I think you saw my article the other day. There's something that's been bothering me,' frowned Rory.

Esko raised an eyebrow and waited.

'If Redetti has been manoeuvring to become Prime Minister,' Rory continued, 'why was Borelli so angry when he left their meeting? I'd assumed it was because she had told him, in her commissioner role, that a new Venetian Republic would have to go through EU membership trials just like a Balkan country.'

'Its old colonies.'

'Just right. But I think there must have been more to it than that.'

Esko grinned. 'Off the record?'

'If it has to be.'

'Just for now.'

'You mean you know?'

'For once I do. It's all thanks to Roberto too. She did tell Borelli that, but it was the Italian, not the European, news that made him furious. Borelli was convinced Redetti would need his vote to pull together a new coalition, so he thought he could threaten her. She offered him a few extra gestures of regional autonomy – one was the right to impose a ten-thousand euro environmental tax on cruise ships entering the Venetian lagoon – but Borelli wanted much more. She told him to get lost. Roberto Vincenzi has agreed to back her, which tips the balance in the Senate in her favour.'

Rory sipped his drink thoughtfully. 'That makes sense. When can I use it?'

'Once you've spoken to Roberto, I expect. You won't have to wait long. Roberto will be delighted to point out to the international press that he is saving Italy and Europe from a constitutional crisis.'

In front of them Amelie had just finished her run, and slithered elegantly to a halt. She was shaking loose her hair and pushing back the goggles. Once her face was revealed she was no longer anonymous. A small posse of photographers was ready for her, and she obliged, adopting all the poses perfected by skiing film stars since the 1950s.

Behind her Nikita arrived with less of a flourish. She was not a woman to be upstaged or ignored, however. Squirting just a slight patina of snow at the lenses of the cameramen, she grabbed hold of Amelie's arm to steady herself.

'Darling, what a run. I had no idea you were so good!'

The smile froze across Amelie's face. 'Now you know. I am.' She bent down to unclip her skis and stalked off to the terrace, leaving Nikita in turn grinning at the retreating photographers.

A minute or two later Artur appeared, descending gently, waiting for Agnestina to catch him up. She rolled alongside him and Arturo circled her with his arm as they drifted to a stop. He waited a moment, pushed her goggles on to her hair and kissed her.

On the terrace Catrina watched. The hint of a smile formed at the corner of her mouth. Suddenly everything was fine again.

The Idea of Shopping

It soon became clear that for Amelie having a quiet lunch on an open terrace with her friends between ski runs was not really an option. Not only was there the incessant clicking of cameras, there was the shameless eavesdropping and videoing on mobile phones, hoping for that gossip-worthy moment worth uploading for the world to gawp at.

'We're going to have to go,' she said apologetically to Nikita as a man attached himself to her ear without warning and thrust a phone in front of her face to take a selfie.

'Darling, it's awful. Couldn't we just move inside?' suggested Nikita.

Amelie shook her head. 'No, they'd just follow. Esko and I will find somewhere less public.'

'If you're going back into town perhaps I could go with you. I might as well write up the interview and file it,' Rory said.

Esko found a taxi and the three of them left the rest of the party to their now uninterrupted lunch, though one or two amateurs hung around at a distance wondering if Nikita and Patrice might be famous after all and worth spying on. Amelie and Esko took the back seats, Rory travelled in front. He ventured to Amelie, turning round, 'I don't suppose you'd like to do an interview with me too?' He wondered if he was pushing his luck, but Amelie showed no sign of irritation.

'Oh, Rory, you are sweet, but I can't, not today. I'm under contract – no press until we finish filming.'

'Fair enough,' said Rory, watching his chance of double glory in the editor's eyes slide away.

'But you shall have an exclusive as soon as I can – in the spring.'

'Fine. Lovely,' he wondered despondently whether he would still be a Brussels journalist by then. There were no guarantees any more – he could almost hear the publisher mouthing those slimy words.

Back at the hotel they separated, each to their rooms, for a room-service lunch, though Amelie announced that they were not to dawdle. She wanted another go on the mountain before the sun hid behind it. Rory resigned himself to hours of writing, by which time everybody would be heading back from the slopes after their day of exhilarating air. His week had been meant to be without duties. Then Redetti and Borelli had turned up. Now suddenly, thanks to them and the

Italian Prime Minister, his weekend would be spent glued to his computer while the others stiffened their thighs against the snow.

On the terrace the others lunched and laughed, but Nikita, who was beginning to regret offering to pay for the whole junket, was feeling spare again. Catrina was in a relieved huddle with Patrice, Artur was making the sort of fishy eyes at Agnestina which signalled the inevitable whack of Cupid's arrow hitting a man in the neck, and Agnestina who, she was now starting to realise, had missed the attention since Flamand walked away, was loving every minute of it.

Mercedes was alone too, of course, but only until Rory had finished writing. Lunch could not go on for ever. Then the pairs of lovers would drift off to the ski lift. For the first time in years Nikita admitted that the idea of shopping bored her. Maybe she could wander the town and discover a private gallery like her own, find out whether there were any artists worth cultivating on show. That way she could persuade herself that at least part of the weekend really was a business trip.

She sighed and her mind wandered back to the kindness of that nice Roberto Vincenzi who had so gallantly rescued her at the airport and bought her clothes, all of which she had still not had time to wear, and the airline had just got around to delivering her diverted suitcase. He had made such an elegant fuss. She wondered whether he was in the neighbourhood. She reached for her handbag. His card was in there still, she was sure.

Composing the text took some thought, but eventually it read:

Roberto my dear, luggage arrived only this morning, don't know what I would have done without you. Still in Bolzano, are you near? Do join if free.

The young couples were starting to drift away. The terrace was losing its charm as cloud drifted in front of the sun. Nikita shivered and, since any answer from Roberto was unlikely to be immediate, decided to move too.

'Mercedes, darling, are you busy?' she asked briskly.

The Spanish woman was a little startled. 'No, I suppose not – not while Rory—'

'Is writing. Exactly. Then let's explore together and research. I'm short of interesting artists for the spring. You never know what we might find.'

In truth Mercedes had been thinking that a little siesta sounded good and that, once he'd filed, Rory could wake her up from it in the delicious way he had yesterday, but it was not a thought to be made public. 'Won't galleries be closed?' she asked.

'Saturday afternoon at the height of the season? Certainly not if they want to survive.'

Mercedes nodded meekly and gave in. 'Of course.'

They had reached the top of the main shopping street and were preparing to turn into one of the more promising and chic side alleys when Nikita's phone burbled. There was a reply from Roberto.

Not today, cara mia. Call me.

Nikita did as she was told. 'What a shame,' she said after they had passed the *pronto* stage. 'We were looking for galleries and new artists and thought what fun it would be to have you with us.'

'A shame indeed,' agreed Roberto, then paused as an idea struck. 'I am leaving Milano now for Roma. Maybe you could join me there? I'm sure the research would be more profitable.'

'Rome!' purred Nikita. 'A lovely idea.'

In his hotel room Rory had finished his article just after four, but by that time the darkness was encroaching outside and Mercedes had returned to warm up. He uploaded the material on to the paper's server. Five minutes later a text arrived:

> Great stuff. Now get your arse to Rome and follow it up. Cheap hotel, mind, and cheaper train fare.

Rory glanced up at Mercedes, wondering how she would take the news. 'I've got to go to Rome in the morning,' he said. 'I thought they'd say that.'

The answer was the last one he expected. 'Perfect! So have I.'

Normal Flagey

As it was the first 'normal' weekend after the New Year holidays, Mariana felt that she should be slipping back into her weekend routine. Unaccountably, however, she was no longer sure what that was – at least, whatever it had been in the old year, she had no desire to replicate it in the new. Before she had gone home to Finland for the holidays weekends in Brussels had been simple enough, if unsatisfactory. The mornings had been spent in Café Franck minding her own business, now and then chatting to Patrice (and, if necessary, Catrina), but mainly keeping a morbid eye on Esko and showering jealous disapproval on Amelie from across the room. After that she would find a worthy cause to champion or study – a yoga workshop, perhaps, or a documentary festival devoted to the impact of malaria, and the next weekend, just to even the score, insects endangered by mass spraying.

Then Bruno had beckoned, and for a fleeting moment she thought that would solve everything – a foolish thought.

Now not only was the main object of her desire and envy out of town, something had shifted in Mariana's psyche as well. The worthy subjects were still worthwhile, but they had lost their masochistic attraction. The beans could grow organically without her. She would still have stern views on distant wars, but no longer felt that her personal fury was the way to end them.

There was the solace of cinema, of course, but since Amelie Poitiers was film personified the whole form was marred by her. The solace would not be sought there. Looking through the window at the frozen lake and ice-rimmed trees did nothing to recommend athletics, and Mariana doubted if she had the dumb loyalty for team sports.

What then? There was only so much time she could squander alone in the café – only so much moping to be endured. Her room at home was a cell and did not beckon. It needed cleaning and the sordid clothes from the last five days needed washing, but the machine could do the latter and cleaning was a Sunday job for a green atheist.

Mariana finished her coffee, adjusted the boa-constrictor scarf and made sure there was a cigarette in her hand for the moment when she crossed the threshold. She missed Damien's nod of farewell and, as she turned left, missed too his amused smile while he watched her light up and pass the windows. The cigarette in her mouth forced her to dawdle and, as she reached the end wall of the Café Franck and the entrance to the main building of the Centre Flagey, she gazed up at the poster for the upcoming events.

Drummin', Strummin', Runnin': An Evening of Plucks, Bangs and Energy from Hungary's Foremost Experimental Physical Music Group was of limited appeal, Mariana decided – so limited that she had trouble imagining who might find it appealing without drugs. Maybe the drugs were crucial. And how many experimental physical music groups could Hungary support in order for there to be a hierarchy? She noticed that she had missed A Night with Nietzsche and would have to wait until Tuesday for the Almost Complete Orchestral Works of Anton Webern, and to find out whether this meant works that were almost complete, missing a movement or two, or that there were some being left out.

On the glass entrance itself was advertised Today 15.00–22.00 and tomorrow at the same time: The Debussy–Fauré Experience. Immerse Yourself in the Songs, Chamber and Orchestral Music of These Two Great French Composers. Mariana shivered, finished her cigarette and was about to glance up at the clock on the church when its bells announced midday. Still three hours to go, then, before she could be immersed by the French. But that thought itself meant that she was decided. She pushed open the door of the box office and booked herself a ticket for both days. Just enough time to go home, eat and change into something more comfortable – or at least in keeping with Mariana's vision of herself as a post-romantic impressionist.

Now she had a purpose.

This was rather more than Saskia van Katwijk had. She too had given up on the joys of café life (café society without acceptable society was dull even to a woman as self-contained as Saskia) and had wandered home up Rue Malibran wondering what to do with the rest of her day. She had collected her now-traditional two bottles of Orvieto from the local convenience shop, as usual exchanging not a word with the man serving her, but even for Saskia just after lunchtime seemed a little early to retreat to her rug with a glass and her computer.

She made herself a true Dutch coffee and a large cheese roll, and scrolled down her phone screen, first to make sure that none of her irritating non-friends had emailed her (no problem, they hadn't), and then to head to the app that would tell her what excitements she could find in Brussels.

Like Mariana she dismissed Hungarian Experimental Physical Music, but unlike her Finnish colleague she had no aversion to film or its stars. She was not the sort to choose any old movie – in fact, the movies as made in Hollywood and its clones would need more than a clever trailer to entice her. What Saskia was looking for was a film that challenged her enough to make her forget her cynicism, that avoided romantic squelch and made her follow a story without once having to bring her acute critical faculties into play. Had she known it (or cared) she and Fidel would have been good cinema companions – neither were impressed by special effects or narrative short cuts, both expected a level of drama that justified the expense of not telling the story in the live theatre.

She stopped scrolling and tapped the screen. This looked possible: *The Month the Blade Sang* – Brazilian film noir with (the publicist couldn't resist adding) a twist. One hundred and thirty minutes and showing in a converted church at the less fashionable end of the town centre – part of a Festival of World Voices.

It was a rather shaken, and slightly shaking, Saskia who emerged from the screening at 9 p.m., and decided that she needed a lot of white wine fast, preferably in a very well-lit bar.

IX

Sunday Again

Almost Triumph

As Catrina and Patrice were having a leisurely Sunday morning breakfast – with Patrice complaining that the Italians, especially the Austrian Italians, had no idea how to make croissants and Catrina countering that in comparison the Belgians had no idea how to make coffee – the thought of going home to Brussels cast a long shadow. Routine loomed too soon.

'You realise we are the only ones going back today,' said Catrina, spearing another pastry filled with apricot.

'Is that right?' Patrice frowned.

'Looks that way. Elise is staying here, of course, and so, naturally, is Fidel. Esko's driving Amelie back to her film shoot and then flying home from Nice. Nikita is diverting to Rome to see her new admirer, Roberto.'

'She lost no time.'

'Nikita is not a woman to waste time on thinking too deeply. And Roberto knows how to shop. Then Rory has been sent to Rome too, following on Roberto's heels thanks to Esko.'

'And so Mercedes goes with him…?'

'Inevitably, but it means she can also scout galleries with Nikita, so it really is business for everybody in Rome.'

'What about Agnestina?'

Catrina watched very carefully how Patrice asked this, and kept analysing every twitch as she answered. 'You saw her and Artur yesterday. It seems it is love at first sight.'

Patrice shrugged. 'Why not? He is a nice boy – and he skis well.'

'So he does.' Catrina was searching for any glimmer, any trace of disappointment in Patrice's face, but he showed none. 'So I expect she'll stay here with Artur, Elise and Fidel for another week.'

Patrice was not just being a good actor. It was part of a barman's identity to flirt a little with his customers, and in the case of Agnestina, the flirting had been in both directions since her brief first-term student fling with Flamand had run out of steam. If she wanted to take up with Elise's brother that was fine too – it just added her to the Café Franck family – and (this was the thought he was not going to share with Catrina) there was rarely a shortage of attractive girls pushing through the curtains to his bar.

For the moment, though, Patrice was perfectly happy with Catrina. He liked her attention, her ready wit, her disorganised prettiness, which made her much more desirable than she realised. With Catrina he had never yet been bored – a lot more than he could say about most people he had come across.

'It's not fair,' said Catrina.

Patrice was puzzled. 'Agnestina and Artur?'

'No, silly. Us being the only ones going home. I suppose it's because we are the only ones with jobs that can't wait.'

'Esko will be in his office tomorrow too. And, you know, this was just a nice gesture from Nikita, not a real holiday.'

'I know but—'

'Maybe next month,' Patrice said, before wandering off to the breakfast buffet for second helpings.

'Next month what?' Catrina asked impatiently, stealing another pastry from his plate as he sat down again.

'Maybe we could find a few days for each other – somewhere warm.'

Catrina paused with the pastry halfway to her mouth. 'You mean it?'

'Certainly.'

She leant across the table and kissed him. 'Yes please.'

Patrice giggled as she sat down.

'What's so funny?'

'Now you have jam on your…'

She looked down and saw exactly where he meant. 'I think you will have to wipe it off upstairs while we pack,' she grinned. 'Quite soon. There's the airport bus at twelve.'

'So soon, darling!' announced Nikita, appearing behind Patrice.

'Afraid so,' said Catrina.

'What a pity you can't come with us to Rome.'

'Yes, it is, isn't it.' Catrina just managed to stop herself adding, 'But some of us have real jobs to get back to.' Instead she put her hand over Patrice's. 'But he says we will make up for it later in the winter and find the sun again.'

'What a man!' Nikita exclaimed, grabbing his other hand.

Patrice squirmed free of both and a muttered a rather more non-committal, 'I will see what can be done,' but winked at Catrina.

'I wanted to say goodbye to Amelie,' said Catrina. 'I'll see Esko at work tomorrow anyway, I expect – unless he doubles back to Rome too. It seems everybody thinks they can be Prime Minister of Italy suddenly.'

'Frankly, darling, they probably can. Amelie's on the mountain, though. She wanted a morning on the slopes before getting in a car again.'

'One more show for the cameras, you mean,' said Catrina.

'Don't be bitchy, darling, you're much nicer than that really.'

'Sorry.'

'And just at the moment they can both do with the publicity. I hear Esko's ex is kicking up quite a fuss in Helsinki and appearing everywhere with her opera singer, so Amelie is proving a point very nicely – and you know a film actress is only as valuable as her last cover feature.'

'I'm so glad I'm not trying to be famous,' said Catrina.

'Yes, it is exhausting,' said Nikita, as if she was trying all the time.

At that moment Amelie's photographic career was experiencing something of a blip. Her progress down the piste was matched on both sides by cameramen with steady cams carefully mounted on their shoulders to give a perfect view of Amelie's lissom progress down the mountain. At the bottom a line of less athletic photographers were strung out across the flat ground waiting to capture the flurry of snow as she slid to a stop and the shaking free of the hair as the goggles were raised in triumph.

Reality was more cruel. She did slide to a stop – not side-on in a flurry of wispy snow, but straight into the chest of the middle snapper.

'Arrrgh!' yelled Amelie. It was a shame that his camera was raised at the time so that the lens went straight into her left goggle. She collapsed to the ground, clasping her eye. Her obstruction fell too, clutching the ruins of his camera. There would be bruises.

Moving On

Silence was usually the prerogative of Finns, thought Esko later as he steered the car elegantly around two lumbering trucks on the autostrada. But for once it was not him who was being stern and silent. He was humming to himself, knowing that it would drive Amelie mad.

She it was who sat tight-lipped, except for an occasional sigh. Behind her dark glasses she glared at the road ahead, daring it, Esko or any other entity on earth to contradict her

Trappist fury. She could feel the flesh around her eye swelling. Presumably it was bruising too. She had no intention of asking Esko the extent of the damage.

Just west of Genoa, as they saw the Mediterranean coast for the first time since Friday morning, Esko hit on Amelie's big worry. It was big in that it was likely to be very expensive. There were other worries – pain, shame, the disaster to her looks and the sheer humiliation of the truth – but this was legal.

'I suppose,' Esko suggested quietly, 'your agent was smart enough to make sure there was no clause against winter sports in your contract?'

The silence continued. Only a slight tightening of Amelie's grip on the knee of her trousers gave the answer.

'Ah,' said Esko, catching the movement, 'unfortunate'.

Back in Bolzano Nikita, rather chastened by the size of the accumulated bill, had been escorted in a taxi to the train station by Mercedes and Rory, who felt more and more like a porter as he struggled with Nikita's combined luggage – combined because her large original suitcase, lost by the airline, had now been supplemented by all the clothes bought for her by Roberto and her own forays into the town's shops. Nikita herself believed in paying, not carrying. As he struggled to load his burdens into the racks at the end of the first-class carriage Rory decided that, whatever deviousness it needed, he was not flying back from Rome to Brussels on the same flight as his benefactor. At least from that morning he was officially on *Europe Now*'s expenses, and could assert his independence without feeling guilty or ungrateful.

Almost exactly a week since Elise had parted company from her snowboard and thudded into the mountainside, she was saying goodbye to the nurses and being helped slowly and a little gingerly towards a waiting taxi. Artur supported her on one side, Agnestina on the other. Fidel had been gently but firmly told in a note from Elise that he was not needed, but perhaps he could arrange a little homecoming for her when she made it to the hotel.

'They seemed so long, the days when I wondered where I was and if I would ever mend. Now it feels like no time at all.'

'There were many hours, signorina,' said a handsome young doctor, gravely shaking her hand, 'when we thought you would not mend. You are very strong.'

'I don't feel it.'

'Another week, maybe two.' He smiled. 'You go back to Brussels today?'

'No, my brother and I have another week of holiday paid for, so we shall stay.'

'In that case, please come and see me on Friday. I will be happy to confirm your progress – but,' he admonished, 'you must be careful – perhaps not too much spumante.'

Elise wondered whether he was metaphorically telling her not to get too excited, or just to be sparing with holiday wine. Relying on the walking stick less than she expected (Artur had swapped the hospital issue with an elegant cane topped by bone carved into the head of a chamois), she made her way into the afternoon sunlight and immediately felt better. She hadn't realised how heavily the artificial light and the hospital atmosphere had been weighing on her spirits.

Bending to fit into the front seat of the taxi was painful, though. Her ribs protested, her legs resisted being folded, her back sank into its new position stiffly and informed her that it would not now wish to change shape for some time. Artur fussed over fixing her seat belt, gave the driver stern instructions for smooth steering and settled himself into the back where Agnestina kissed him approvingly.

In the hotel lobby Fidel had been busy, determined to prove that his days of uselessness were over. His sprained ankle was healing too, his bandages had been removed, replaced with an elastic support stocking, and he had trained himself to manoeuvre around on his crutches, if not with the nimbleness of a dancer, at least with confident efficiency.

In a corner of the lobby a table had been set with two vases of flowers, a tower of cream cakes and an ice bucket holding the best Prosecco the manager could find – from his uncle's own cellars, he had promised Fidel, putting the family honour at stake.

Indeed the hotel had heard every twist and turn of Elise and Fidel's misfortunes, and now Agnestina's appropriation of Artur too, so this tea without tea was as much their contribution to the homecoming as Fidel's. Very much better rooms had been arranged for all at no extra cost, for the hotel had also been visited by Amelie and Esko when they crossed the road to say goodbye to Fidel. Amelie had even been gracious enough to sign the visitor's book. That alone made the manager dream of his new entry on the booking websites. It was the closest his career came to bliss.

Fidel enveloped Elise in his arms as she came through the doors, their stick and crutches clattering so that only the steadying hand of Artur stopped them both toppling to the marble floor.

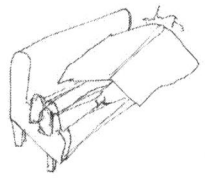

Therapies

On Sunday morning Bruno discovered the ultimate duplicity of Tyron Wangstrutt. Had he been close enough to Saskia to complain, she would have sniffed and told him that that was exactly the sort of betrayal she would have expected of an Overijssel Wangstrutt. As it was, it was just Bruno who sniffed. Then he sneezed, groaned, blew his nose and sniffed again. TW had not caught his cold from Bruno, but the latter was as sure as Houston was hot the wretched man had passed it on. In theory it could have attacked Bruno as a result of his chill a week earlier – falling in the snow, lowering his immunity with too much *vin chaud* and then standing in the queue outside Parliament in the freezing cold. That seemed too generous an explanation.

Bruno cursed the man from Missouri, but even the curses were ineffectual when broken up by sneezes. The only plus side was that he had stocked up with British concoctions of extra-power analgesic hot blackcurrant at home over Christmas, knowing some germ would strike sooner or later. He made an Arctic expedition to the kitchen, stopped halfway to turn up the thermostat, boiled a kettle and added to the paracetamol mixture a generous slug of cheap whisky. Shivering with fever he made the return journey to bed like a climber finding Base Camp. The duvet was pulled over his head; it would only be lowered to drink, reach for a tissue or, Bruno thought, either death or spring released him.

TW himself was back on form. He had slogged back the attacks coming from California by ringing through at an hour on Saturday when he knew his superiors would be in the yard building the barbecue or grilling themselves on the beach. He had explained the temperature in Brussels and his symptoms in gruesome detail, making his ordeal on the eleventh floor of Hotel Dutoit sound like the martyrdom of St Sebastian.

He had also, as with Bruno the day before, deflected the blame for the Parliament's admonishment away from him. How was he to know, he bleated to Ziggie Industries' Vice-President for Public Affairs (Global), that executives at Head Office would be so stupid as to send him on an important mission without covering the regulatory basics? He reminded the VP that he was contract, not staff, and threatened to add his own legal suit, alleging reputational damage to Wangstrutt Associates, to the substantial pile of litigation already obscuring the corporation's desks.

The upshot was very satisfactory from TW's point of view. He would spend the rest of the month in the Hotel Dutoit, expenses unlimited, doing his best to retrieve the situation Ziggie, not he, had put themselves in.

Debussy and Fauré had meant nothing to Mariana before Saturday – at least, they had meant no more than pleasant tunes and enjoyable background music when she wanted to wear headphones: when running, for example. Completely to her surprise, drifting into the immersion weekend in the concert hall of the Flagey Arts Centre had changed all that. Mariana was a woman who liked immersion, and once immersed she concentrated.

As she showered the next morning (a long and luxurious process on a Sunday) she reflected that for the first part of the session she had thought Debussy's music much superior and intriguing, with its harmonic twists and turns, its melodic diversions – and Fauré's too late romantic and timid. But then, in the evening, when the focus had switched to Fauré's piano quartets, she had realised how fierce and beautiful he could be; as the pianist had explained, 'energy without shouting, passion without melodrama'. That is how she would like to be thought of herself, she pondered as she towelled dry, then (catching a glimpse in the mirror) wondered if she really was too thin. Maybe the energy would be dismissed as nerves.

The second day of musical immersion promised songs before lunch, piano music after and a full orchestra and choir in the evening. There was just time before the singing began for croissants filled with cheese and ham in the food market on Place Flagey and an American-size cappuccino, though she could not quite bring herself to add sugar.

Watching Mariana without really seeing her as she crossed the tram tracks, Flamand sipped his bitter black coffee and felt Agnestina's absence keenly. Perhaps he had been too hasty to walk away, too clever when he ignored her, too pugnaciously provocative when he had flaunted his other friends at her. He wondered where she was and if there was anything he could do about it. The simple answer was he should ask her. But he needed courage for that. In yet another departure from habit he went to the bar, refused Damien's offer of more coffee, and bought himself a neat vodka. One turned out not to be enough, but after the second he pressed the call icon and rang her.

Since Agnestina was at that moment deciding whether to risk full speed or to snow-plough more gently down the mountainside, there was no answer. Flamand did not leave a message. He waited an hour then sent a text.

This time only ten minutes went by before a reply came through.

OK. In Italy. One week. Ax

Flamand was ridiculously thrilled. She had replied. She was on holiday, not deliberately avoiding Café Franck or him, and she would be back.

He would have been a lot less happy if he had seen Arturo helping her out of her ski suit at the end of the sporting day. He would have been perturbed, too, by her next text – to Heinke, Gräfin von Starnberg – explaining that she would not after all be coming through Munich immediately, but would the following Sunday be possible? The Gräfin too was promptly delighted. Agnestina had three hearts fluttering simultaneously.

When Catrina and Patrice parted at the Trôn metro station back in Brussels to catch separate buses to their respective tiny flats in different zones of Ixelles, Patrice thought he would be relieved. He imagined being able once again to fall back into his inconsequential routine as a single man with an occasional girlfriend, sleeping alone before the early morning shift in Flagey started the week. He was therefore as surprised as Catrina when, two hours later, he rang her doorbell and, as nonchalantly as could, asked to stay the night.

It was Catrina who had the momentary panic, having just emptied the whole week's washing on to the floor. In the end she shrugged, told him to go and buy wine while she tidied up, and preened with pleasure as she decided that the dark clothes would be first into the machine.

First thing on Monday morning, before he dressed and headed for Parliament, Esko phoned Amelie, fully expecting either a continuation of her furious silence or, if not the silence, just the fury itself.

'Hallo, darling,' Amelie answered brightly.

'Everything OK?' Esko ventured tentatively.

'Absolutely.'

'How is your eye?'

'Black, oh so black – except where it is yellow – and blue.'

'The director isn't shouting, the lawyers are not ready to pounce?'

'Oh no, nothing like that.'

'Um... why not?'

'Well, it was easy really. We just decided to rewrite scene twenty and twenty-one this morning. Now there will be a fight, some violence in scene twenty. We will just film out of sequence – like we often do – but with less make-up.'

'Of course – naturally.' Esko rang off. Why couldn't politics be like that, he mused – just a story told out of sequence?

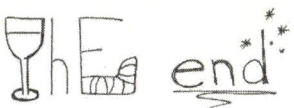

until spring